Richard S. Greenough

Arabesques

Monarè. Apollyona. Domitia. Ombra

Richard S. Greenough

Arabesques
Monarè. Apollyona. Domitia. Ombra

ISBN/EAN: 9783743304963

Manufactured in Europe, USA, Canada, Australia, Japa

Cover: Foto ©Andreas Hilbeck / pixelio.de

Manufactured and distributed by brebook publishing software
(www.brebook.com)

Richard S. Greenough

Arabesques

ARABESQUES:

MONARÈ.   DOMITIA.

APOLLYONA.   OMBRA.

BY

MRS. RICHARD S. GREENOUGH,

AUTHOR OF "LADY TREMYSS; OR, TREASON AT HOME."

BOSTON:

ROBERTS BROTHERS.

1872.

CONTENTS.

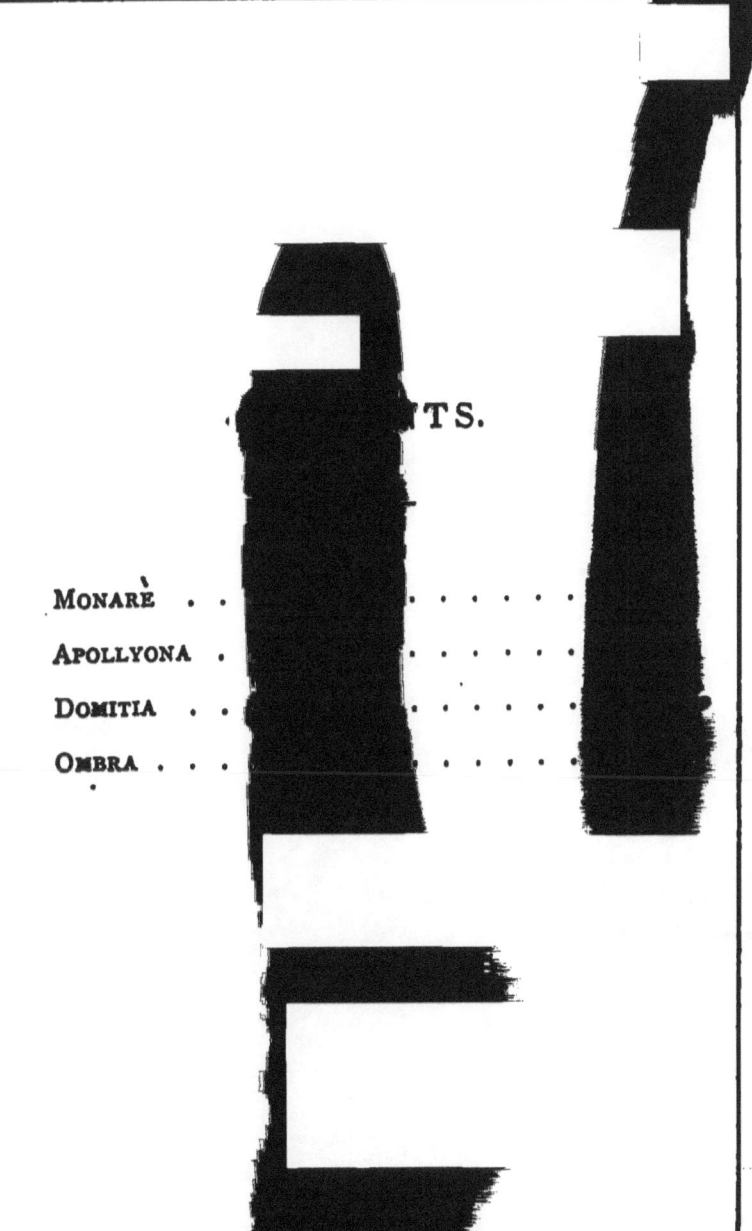

MONARÈ.

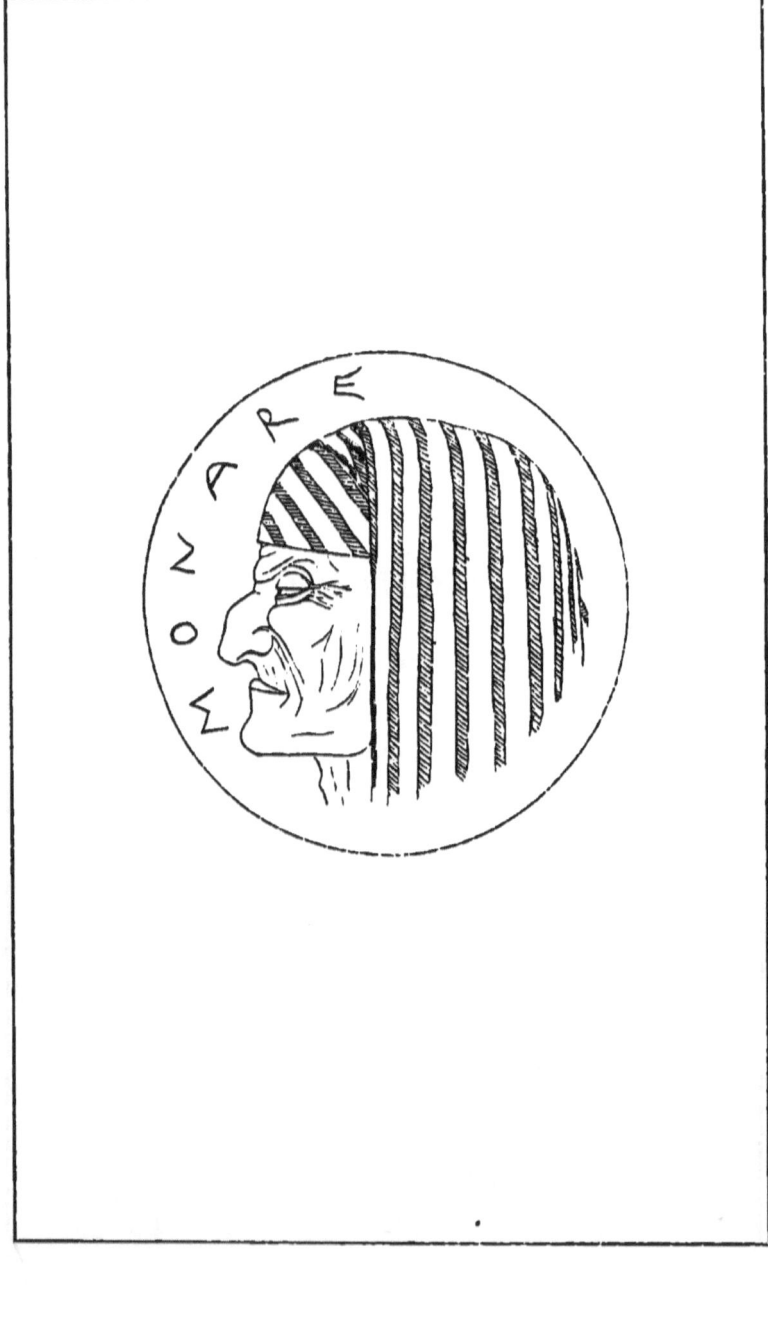

MONARÈ.

IGHT had fallen, covering the broad stretch of the plain with shadow. The little huts which clustered around the massive castle of Ilzerley were hidden from sight; and the presence of the castle itself could be perceived only from a long, pale ray of light which streamed from a narrow window, the window of the chapel where Walter of Ilzerley kept his vigil, watching his armor, for the next day was to see him dubbed a knight.

The castle was filled with lords and ladies from all the country round, come to assist at to-morrow's ceremony. There had been feasting and revelling, dance and song; but now all had retired to rest ; and the young man knelt before the altar, companioned by solemn thoughts alone.

The chapel was narrow and high ; from niches on either side grim effigies of saints looked down ; ranged on either hand stood the suits of armor of the past lords of Ilzerley, each guarding as it were his own tomb. The pavement was worn and uneven. Overhead swung an iron lamp, suspended by a chain. It lighted but faintly the gloom of the chapel ; its rays seemed gathered together upon Walter's form as he knelt below it, and were reflected from his snowy vest and curling golden hair.

He knelt and prayed that he might be strengthened worthily to fulfil the vows he was to take on the morrow. He thought of the long line of ancestors from whom he was descended, and his heart burned to emulate their noble deeds. He thought of the woe and wickedness that divided the earth between them ; and he longed to grasp his knightly sword to do battle for the oppressed. And as he mused and prayed alternately, the night wore on.

It was at the deepest and the darkest when a low wind swept through the chapel, and waved the banners on the wall. He thought he heard a sad human wail, but the wind died away. He listened. There was no sound. Again he mused

and prayed, and again the wind swept through
the chapel, louder, stronger than before; and it
bore with it the sound of a woman's voice wailing, —

"Who shall deliver me from this captivity?"

Walter of Ilzerley started to his feet. He felt
the golden curls rising on his head; but his heart
was stout and firm, overflowing the while with
tender ruth and compassion.

"Lo, here I stand, Walter of Ilzerley, whom
to-morrow will see dubbed a knight; and I will
strive, so help me God, to deliver thee from thy
captivity."

And as he spoke, a chorus of voices, from the
suits of armor of the dead lords standing around,
responded: —

"We attest the vow."

And eyes looked steadfastly from the eye-holes
of the before empty helmets, and the steel-clad
and gauntleted right arms were raised, as if
invoking the witness of God's sight, while the
banners above waved solemnly, as if conscious
of the vow. As the sound of the voices died
away, a ruby ring fell at Walter of Ilzerley's feet.
As it struck on the pavement before him, the
flame of the lamp flickered and went out: but
he was not left in darkness; a rosy light flashed
from the ring, and filled the chapel with a soft

radiance. It gleamed on the iron armor, on the stone saints, on the torn and time-stained banners, and on Walter's awe-struck face. He raised it and placed it on his hand; then, kneeling before the altar, he prayed, with earnestness unknown before, that God would grant him wisdom, valor, and patience to rescue from her captivity the lady who had called him to her aid.

The next day came, and with great pomp and solemnity the gray-headed old Count of Lestuys gave him the knightly accolade, and the two fairest damsels of the assemblage buckled on his golden spurs, and tied his scarf across his breast.

Great preparations had been made for feasting for many days. Minstrels and harpers had flocked to the castle; the pantry and buttery were filled to overflowing with mighty pasties, huge loaves of manchet bread, and great baskets of cakes made with spices and honey. Casks of the oldest and strongest wines were broached, and all was gladness and gayety. But the midnight voice sounded ever in Walter's ear, with its complaint, —

" Who shall deliver me from this captivity? "

He looked at the ruby ring. Its rays seemed hour by hour to pale. He determined to delay no longer, but to set forth that very afternoon.

So while all the guests were assembled in the
great hall, listening to the minstrels who were
singing, turn by turn, the romance of Gui de
Provens, he mounted his white horse, took his
shield on which he had that day ordered the de-
vice of a ring to be painted with the motto, " I
seek ; " and, without bidding adieu to any one,
he crossed the drawbridge, and went on his way.

As his gallant white steed passed across the
creaking and groaning bridge, he tossed his head
and snorted cheerily ; and the ruby ring on Walter of Ilzerley's finger sent forth rays so brilliant
that he could scarcely bear to look at it. They
lay like a rosy line of light before him ; and those
whom he met shaded their eyes with their hands,
and said, —

" Mort de St. Denis ! that young knight's armor
shines so bright that one can't look at him."

For they did not know that it was the ruby
ring that dazzled them.

He journeyed on all that day. The land was
sad and sterile. At intervals rose dark and
frowning fortresses, each with a little settlement
of huts around it. In the immediate neighborhood of these strongholds he saw cultivated
fields, horses and cattle peacefully grazing ; but
it seemed as if neither peasant nor animal dared
venture outside that narrow circuit. The ground

between was bare and wild. Ever and anon he would pass an abbey or convent with its towers and its ample domain. There he saw more thrift, wider fields and fairer crops; but there were few of these, not enough to redeem the look of desert solitude of the country.

As night drew on, he found himself on a bleak and sullen sweep. The earth looked as though fire had passed over it, and had left it strewn with ashes. Dismal fogs rose in the distance, and slowly crept forward as if to meet and encircle him. His horse turned his head towards his master and neighed plaintively, as if asking where they were to find shelter. Walter of Ilzerley looked anxiously at his ring as for guidance. As his eye rested on it, it shot forth a long ray that pierced the gathered fog and showed, on a small eminence before him, a low, gray hut. The young man cheered his horse with his voice, and raised him with the bridle; and, avoiding as he best might the pools filled with brackish water which were scattered over the plain, he pressed forward towards the solitary gray hut.

As he approached it, a towering form, clothed in a knight's surcoat, appeared at the door.

"Good knight, I crave your hospitality for the dark hours," said the young man.

"Such as I have to offer is yours," replied the knight in a deep, hoarse voice. And he drew near the steed, as the rider dismounted, stretching out his hand as if to take the bridle. But as he advanced, the horse trembled in every limb, laid his ears close to his head, and started back cowering. The knight turned on his heel without remarking the strange behavior of the steed, and led the way to a sort of cave behind the eminence.

"You will find fodder and water within," he said.

The cave was dark; but the ruby ring lighted its every corner, and showed a clear stream trickling from a rock on one side, and a pile of dried grass.

The knight stood silent at the door while the young man rubbed down and caressed his tired steed. Then, when these kind offices were accomplished, he bade him follow.

He conducted Walter into the hut, which was furnished with a strange mixture of poverty and of luxury. On the rough wooden table lay a cloth broidered with hawks and hounds; on rude shelves stood silver flagons; and on the earthen floor was laid a carpet from Eastern looms. But, peculiar as were these things, Walter of Ilzerley's attention was still more powerfully attracted by a strange odor which pervaded the hut, — a smell as of some wild animal. He glanced around to see whether his host had not some slaughtered creature near. But nothing was to be seen.

The host bade Walter be seated, and gave him bread and wine.

"I have no meat to offer you," he said; and, as he spoke, his eyes grew small and green, he half smiled, and showed white, pointed teeth.

Walter of Ilzerley looked keenly at him; but the knight's eyes were as they had been before, and the points had vanished from his teeth.

"No meat is needed," said Walter; and he crossed himself and gave thanks ere he broke the bread.

The knight breathed hard, and drops stood on his forehead, as he heard the holy words.

When the young man had ended his frugal supper, he arose and requested his host to show him where he was to sleep. The hermit knight drew aside a heavy curtain and revealed a small inner room wherein was a low bed, and bade him sleep, and sleep soundly. His eyes again grew small and green as he spoke; and, as he smiled, he showed again white, pointed teeth.

Walter of Ilzerley knelt before his cross-hilted sword, and, having prayed, took off his armor and lay down upon the low pallet. For some time he could not sleep. The strange odor, as of some wild animal, seemed to taint and poison the air. But at length weariness overcame him, and his eyelids closed.

He was wakened by a vivid flash like lightning across his eyes. He started to his feet, and instinctively grasped the sword which he had laid beside him. The ruby was sending forth fiery darts, and showed, below the heavy curtain of the entrance, the head and shoulders of an enormous wolf, with green eyes, and pointed, glistening teeth. Walter of Ilzerley sprang towards the animal, and smote upon its hairy, bristling neck with his good sword.

A human shriek rent the air; the monster changed before his horror-stricken sight; and there at his feet, the blood pouring from a ghastly wound in his throat, lay the knight who had bidden him welcome, — a were-wolf.

The young man stood for a moment without speech or motion; then he took from the shelf in the next room a tall, long-necked silver flagon, and filled it with the smoking blood; for in those days every one knew that a drop of the blood of a were-wolf, which never curdles, would bring to life his victims, no matter how long they had been dead. This being done, he had no mind

to tarry longer in the dead monster's den ; and
so he saddled and bridled his horse, and rode
away over the dark plain.

As the day began to break, he saw, rising from
the surface of the plain, large heaps of white
stones surmounted by wooden crosses. Most of
them seemed to have been there for a long time,
but one of them was freshly erected. As he approached, he saw, crouching on the ground beside it, a little boy. The young man's heart
melted at the sight of the desolate child crouching on the ground damp with the night dew.
He drew near. As the child heard the horse's
steps, he looked up and showed a face pale with
weeping.

" My child, what brings you here?" said the
young knight. " Where is your home, and where
are your parents? "

" I have no home. There lies my only parent,
killed by the were-wolf, like all the rest," said
the child ; and he sobbed and wept aloud.

Walter of Ilzerley descended from his horse,
and, raising the silver flagon, poured from it one
drop upon the stones.

Immediately the heap quaked, and was rent
asunder, and forth came a man whole and un-
harmed, rubbing his eyes like one aroused from
slumber.

"Why, Tristam, my son, I wake from an ugly dream. I thought the were-wolf had me. — But what makes you look so pale?" said the man as he patted the head of the child, who was staring at him with widely opened eyes, and cheeks paler than before.

The little boy did not speak, for he was too much frightened; but the young knight told him all that had happened; whereupon the man knelt down and thanked God and Walter of Ilzerley alternately.

The knight gave the man half of the blood, and bade him let fall one drop of it on all the heaps of stones; he charged him also to say himself, and to bid all that the wolf's blood should bring to life to say, three Pater-nosters every morning and every evening for his success in the expedition on which he was bound; then he rode away where the ruby light pointed.

As he reached the border of the plain, he looked back, and saw a kneeling crowd; and, as he strained his ear, the morning wind brought to him the sound of their prayer and praise. And his heart was glad within him, and he journeyed on in the sweet light of the sun, over fields fair with flowers and glittering with dew. Little birds sang on the trees, and the May flies and butterflies sported around him, as he rode on his way, singing an old song of knightly valor and of ladies' grace.

The sun was high overhead when he saw in the distance a castle by the sea. As he came towards it, he saw that it was broad and high, and looked as if it were the residence of some mighty lord; but no knightly banner floated from its walls. A large black pennon drooped sadly against its staff. Walter of Ilzerley rode forward and sounded the horn which hung ready for the use of travellers. A head appeared at the small grated window in the gate, and the porter asked who sounded, and what was his errand.

"Walter of Ilzerley am I called, and my errand is to redress a great wrong," answered the young knight.

"Tarry awhile till I ask what is my lady's will concerning you," said the porter; and he retired from the grate, leaving the traveller much surprised at such an uncourteous reception. He looked around as he sat on his steed waiting. The peasants of the surrounding cottages were busy at their toil in the fields. They were more hale and cheerful than most of their class. They looked well fed and well cared for, but each man wore a black band upon his right arm; and the women and girls, whom he saw busy at their household tasks, all wore black caps and scarfs. Yet they talked and laughed gayly, and seemed to pay no heed to the gloomy tokens they bore.

His marvelling was interrupted by the rattling of the chains that supported the drawbridge, and the groaning of the portcullis as it was raised to admit him. He rode forward. As he entered the court-yard, he perceived that the porter and all the retainers were dressed in black. At the extremity of the court, on the lowest step of a broad flight of stone stairs, stood the seneschal, a venerable, white-bearded man, clothed in black like the rest.

"Welcome, Walter of Ilzerley," he said; "my lady awaits you."

The young knight dismounted, much astonished at all he saw.

He followed the seneschal up the broad stone stairs into a long and lofty room. On either side sat a row of young girls spinning. At the upper end of the room, on a raised dais, sat the lady. She had 'been beautiful; but sorrow had furrowed her forehead, and quenched the brightness of her eyes. She rose as the young knight approached, and extended her hand.

"Welcome, Walter of Ilzerley," she said; "welcome to a doubly smitten house, — a house reft of its lord and of its child."

"Were your sorrow, lady," answered the young knight, "such as admitted of human aid, then would I bind myself to your service so soon as my present errand be fulfilled; but against such grief as yours the bravest arm lies helpless. I can but grieve with you."

The lady turned to an old priest who sat in the deep embrasure of the window behind her, reading his breviary, and who had not even raised his head at the young man's entrance.

"Father Anselm," she said, "tell this stranger the story of my woe. Perhaps it may be granted to him to succeed in that enterprise wherein those that preceded him have failed."

At these words all the black-robed maidens stopped their spinning, and fastened their eyes sorrowfully on the young knight, and sighed. It was as if a low wind had swept through the hall, and brought back to Walter of Ilzerley's memory the midnight wail in the chapel.

The old priest closed his book, and rose, turning towards the youth.

"My blessing be upon you, my son," he said. "The lady's will shall be obeyed. Follow me to my cell. There will I tell you what grievous woe rests upon this house."

Walter saluted the lady, glanced at the rows of black-robed maidens, who with bowed heads were again busy at their wheels, and retired with the old priest. He followed him through dark, winding passages, cut in the thickness of the stone wall, into his cell; narrow, but lighted by a window which looked out upon the sea. On a little wooden table stood a crucifix and a skull; and the stone floor before it was worn into a hollow where the knees of the good priest had been pressed in his hours of prayer.

"Be seated, my son," said Father Anselm, as he drew forward a wooden stool, and offered it to the youth. He sat down himself upon the low truckle-bed, folded his hands, and heaved a deep sigh. After a pause, during which Walter pondered what grief this might be, and what courage and fortune might be necessary to remove it, the old priest thus began: —

"Do not think, my son, that this castle was always the gloomy abode that you now see it. I remember when troops of lords and ladies made it gay with jest and song from morn till midnight. Every day there was hunting and hawking, tilting and jousting; for the count and countess were young, and loved pleasure, like all the young and fortunate. Good were they, and pious also; and on the first day of every month, they and all their guests and all their household, carrying lighted tapers, walked

2

in solemn procession to the shrine of St. Mary
of Aspramont, a league away, on the high hill
that overhangs the sea.

"It was fourteen years ago, — I shall never
forget that glad and sunny morning which was
to have so black a close, — fourteen years ago
the drawbridge was lowered, and forth walked
Count Egbert in his gorgeous dress, leading by
her hand his lady all blazing with gold and
jewels, both bearing great waxen tapers half an
ell high. And all the lords and ladies, magnificently attired and bearing lighted tapers also,
and all the household, followed, save two or
three old servants who were too infirm to walk
so far, and the count and countess' little daughter, their only child, a babe a twelvemonth old,
with her nurse. The nurse stood on the lower
step of the great stone stairs, and held the child
in her arms; and the little thing sprang and
laughed for joy as she saw the goodly company
and the lighted tapers pass by. Each lord and
lady saluted her and bade her good-by as they
passed; for she was a sweet and gracious child,
and all loved her. Her father and mother
looked back and smiled and beckoned with their
hand at her as they left the court-yard; but they
did not dream that that was to be their last look
on their little one.

" The procession passed over the drawbridge and through the pleasant fields, chanting St. Mary's hymn as they went. The sweet voices of the ladies and the deep tones of the knights sounded as though nightingales were singing beside the swelling sea.

" Strange was it that the moment which saw the count and countess bent on such pious intent should have brought to them the misery of their lives. As they rose from their knees before the shrine, one of the knights looked towards the sea and shouted, ' Holy Virgin, the pirates ! '

" They all rushed to the edge of the cliff; and there, below them, they saw a great Saracenic galley just entering the bay before the castle. The ladies shrieked and knelt, all save the countess. She snatched the dagger from her husband's belt, and sprang down the steep. The count and all the knights and retainers followed, bounding like deer over the stones, down the broken and rugged way, the countess before them. The way was long, — too long. The castle was hid from their sight by the thick wood. They darted through its shadows, and came out upon the sunny plain. The pirates were already in their boats. Ere the knights could reach the shore, they had gained their vessel; the wind was filling her sails and bearing them away.

" The countess had flown towards the castle.
As her husband and his friends, baffled, for they
had no vessel wherewith to chase the pirates,
crossed the drawbridge which had been left
lowered for their return, they saw the murdered
bodies of the old servants stretched upon the
reddened stones of the court-yard.

" ' My child!' cried the count in a tone of
anguish ; and he rushed towards his little daughter's room. It was empty of child and nurse.
On the floor lay the countess, still and white as
though dead. They brought her back to life
with much labor and pains ; but from that day
neither she nor her husband ever smiled again,
nor did they ever renew their pilgrimage to St.
Mary's shrine, which was a great wrong to the
saint. They shut themselves up in their private
apartments, and mourned without ceasing. No
more mirth or song enlivened the castle, and
hospitality was given to strangers for one night
only. They brooded over their loss till they
fancied themselves aggrieved by Providence ;
and they had no thought for the still greater
distresses of the poor around them, who that
year, for it was a year of famine, saw their children perishing before their eyes for lack of
food.

"Another great misery befell on that year. It

was the appearance of the were-wolf, which has ever since desolated the country."

At the mention of the were-wolf, the young man bent forward and listened still more attentively.

" The Sieur Nicolas de Maupré was a haughty and lawless lord, whose chief occupation was in waylaying travellers, and his chief pleasure in torturing them until they were fain to ransom themselves at the cost of all they possessed. This wicked lord, as I say, one day disappeared ; and no one could imagine what had become of him, until many others disappeared also, and the rumor spread in the country that a were-wolf had taken up its abode near by. Then every one knew. that the wicked knight had turned himself into a were-wolf; and all the people since then have lived in terror of their lives, and many have been destroyed in spite of all their precautions ; for there lives no beast or being so treacherous, so wily, and so cruel, as the were-wolf. Anathema maranatha !"

And the priest crossed himself.

" But I must go on, and bring my sorrowful history to its close. One afternoon the count wandered forth across the meadows on a solitary walk. Hours passed, the evening meal was ready to be served, but he did not return.

The countess was at prayers in the chapel, and did not perceive her lord's absence; but those of the household began to feel uneasy. They were all watching if they could catch sight of the count returning, when in the dusky twilight they beheld the figure of a boy running towards the castle. As he reached the walls, he shouted, —

" 'The count! the were-wolf!' and sank down upon the stones.

" All the retainers seized torches and weapons and rushed forth in search of their master, taking courage from their numbers; for not one of them, much as they loved their lord, would have dared venture out alone with the chance of meeting the monster.

" Guided by the lad's directions, they sought and found a little brook which ran babbling down from a steep rock into the sea; and on its bank lay all that remained of the count. He had fought manfully against the beast, as the torn and trampled ground proved; but what can one mortal man do against a were-wolf?

" With groans and sobs the retainers took up their lord's remains and bore them to the castle; and not one of them but wept like a child when the countess met them ere they reached the drawbridge. I will not describe her grief. One should have seen it to know what it was.

"The count was buried in the chapel, before the altar; and there three times a day, at morning and noon and night, the countess kneels, and listens to a mass for the dead. And her affliction has borne good fruit. She spends all the rest of her time in caring for the sick, the poor, and the afflicted; deeming her second bereavement a chastisement sent from heaven because of the rebellious manner in which she received the first. And all the country around blesses her, and grieves because of her grief.

"But now, my son, I must leave you, unless, indeed, you will accompany me to the chapel; for noon is at hand, and I must say the mass for the dead."

"One instant, my father," said Walter of Ilzerley; "tarry one instant. Surely by the hand of superhuman wisdom was I brought hither."

And the young knight told the priest how he had slept in the den of the were-wolf, and had slain him, and had brought away his blood. And the old man lifted up his hands and thanked Heaven, while tears of joy ran down his withered cheeks and dropped on his brown robe. Then he led Walter to the chapel, and bade him stand at the foot of the count's tomb.

He had scarcely taken his place there when the countess appeared, followed by all her ser-

vants and retainers, and knelt to listen to the
mass. But, instead of the service for the dead,
the old priest chanted out, in a broken voice, a
canticle of thanksgiving. The countess and all
her servants were greatly astonished; the more
so that they saw the young knight standing with
a joyful face, holding a silver flagon upraised in
his hand.

When the priest had ended the canticle, he
said in a loud voice, —

" Daughter, arise and rejoice. The days of
thy mourning are ended."

Thereupon Walter of Ilzerley poured a drop
of the were-wolf's blood upon the tomb. And
the tomb opened in the middle, and the count
arose and came forth, shading his eyes with his
hand, as one whom a sudden light wakens. And
the chapel was filled with the cries of fright and
joy of all the servants and retainers; but the
count and countess spake never a word, but
stood fast locked in each other's arms.

That night bonfires blazed so broad and high
from the walls of the castle, that they reddened
the whole sky; and troops of horsemen from
all the fortresses for fifteen miles around came
hurrying to see what had happened, and to offer
their aid. They were all bid right welcome;
and oxen were roasted whole, and a great row

of wine-casks was brought up from the cellars, and broached and ran without stint or measure. As each successive troop came into the court-yard, and were met by the joyful news, they set up such a shout of joy that it echoed from the castle walls far over the meadows and back to the distant hills. Never was there known such gladness and revelling.

But Walter of Ilzerley, when the evening meal was ended, retired from the great hall, bright with the blaze of a hundred torches, and glad with the voices of the count and countess' fast arriving friends, and took his stand upon the walls and looked towards the dark, scarce seen sea, wondering what errand it might be that he was to undertake at the countess' behest when his present enterprise should be ended. He was standing, his eyes fixed upon the ruby ring which shone brightly on his hand, but shot forth no guiding ray, when Father Anselm approached him, and begged that he would deign to follow to the presence of the count and countess.

He found them in a small, round room, built in one of the towers. In the middle of the floor stood a child's cradle, the bedclothes tossed here and there in confusion, as if the little creature had been but just snatched up. Around were strewn little playthings; and on a chair lay a child's embroidered dress, but every thing looked old and tarnished.

The countess was standing, her hand clasped in her husband's, her face buried on his shoulder. She raised her head as the young knight entered, and he saw that she had been weeping. The count's face also was sad and sorrowful. The lady spoke.

"Walter of Ilzerley, God knows whether or not I am grateful to you for what you have done this day. Not because I lightly esteem the service already rendered do I sue you for another boon. Father Anselm has told you of our child. Nothing in this room has been touched since she was stolen from it. Each night of these long years have I come hither to mourn for my darling. Two months ago, I was kneeling here at midnight, when I heard a soft low wind come sweeping over the sea, and it bore to my ears my daughter's voice wailing, —

"'Who shall deliver me from this captivity?'"

When Walter of Ilzerley heard these words, the blood rushed in a mighty column to his heart, and his breath stopped; but he was silent, and the lady went on : —

"Since then two knights have come to this castle, and to each have I told my daughter's prayer. Each has ridden away on the morrow in search of her. From that quest neither has returned. But I feel that to you, perhaps, may be granted what has been denied to the other twain; and I implore you, Walter of Ilzerley, by all that you hold dear in this world and the next, to hear a mother's prayer, and pity a mother's anguish."

And so saying, the countess knelt before the young man's feet, and raised her clasped hands, beseeching him.

Walter of Ilzerley raised the lady, and swore never to return to Christian lands till he had found the maiden, and delivered her from the captivity wherein she was bound.

Then the count grasped him by the hand, and said, —

"Young knight, great as is my debt to you, it is as nought to that which it will be when you restore to me my child. And when she is given back to us, should your eyes love to rest upon her, we will give her to you, as your wife, and she shall have a dowry meet for a king's daughter."

But Walter of Ilzerley still kept silence on the voice that had come to him in the midnight chapel, for he felt as if it would be parting with a precious thing, were any save himself to know of it.

He thought of the maiden all that night, nor

had he once closed his eyes to sleep, when the first red streaks of morning shone in the eastern sky. But he felt no fatigue, so bent was his mind upon freeing the count's daughter. He arose, and put on his armor, and, taking leave of the count and countess, he mounted his white·horse, and rode away; while all the retainers bade him adieu, and shouted, "God speed you, brave knight," as he crossed the drawbridge, and came out upon the open plain.

The morning sun shone bright overhead, and the little white clouds floated on the soft blue of the sky, like fairy vessels on a waveless sea. The water danced and sparkled in the light, and the hum of the busy insects, as they flew from flower to flower, filled the air with pleasant sounds. The ruby light lay like a crimson path over the glittering water, and was lost in the distance of the glancing waves.

The knight reined up his horse upon the yellow beach, and looked around for a boat. In a little creek near by he saw a skiff, which two fishermen were dragging into the water.

"Friends, name your price," said the knight, "but I must have your boat."

"It is worth two pieces of gold to us," said the fishermen. The knight gave them four, and, mounting into the little boat with his horse, he pushed off to sea, following the crimson track.

A gentle wind drove forward the skiff, so that the knight had no need to ply the oars. He sat in the stern, his armor flashing back the sunlight; his eyes fixed on the distance where the crimson light pointed; his face full of manly courage, yet soft with tender thought.

Three days and three nights did he, with his good steed, float over the sea, borne on by the gentle wind which never varied nor died away; and, on the morning of the fourth day, he saw the minarets and gilded cupolas of a great city on the shore before him. As he floated nearer, he saw the accursed crescent flashing from every high point, and he knew that he had reached the country of the infidels. Suddenly the ruby light vanished, and a shadow seemed to fall upon him. He looked around. The sun was shining brightly as before; but the reflection of his own figure, of his horse, and of the boat, had disappeared, and he saw that he, and all that belonged to him, had become invisible. The boat pressed forward till it reached the shore; and Walter of Ilzerley, leaping from it, knelt on the sands, and thanked Heaven for having brought him so far safely on his way, and implored its assistance in what he had yet to accomplish; then mounting his horse, he turned towards the bronze gates of the city.

As he passed through the portal, a blind beggar, sitting beside the way, held out his hand and begged for alms.

"Fool," said a tall negro who was lounging in the sunshine, "hold your peace. No one comes this way."

The blind man answered, —

"I know by the measured trembling of the ground that a horse and rider are passing by."

But the negro could see nothing; and he called to his comrades that the blind man had better eyes than they, for that he could perceive a horse and rider where there was nothing but dust and sunshine. And they all laughed and jeered at the blind man.

The young knight left them behind, and went on through the crowded street that lay before him. It was shaded from the heat of the sun by awnings of crimson silk, which were stretched across from the tops of the houses; and beneath were endless rows of stalls filled with gorgeous silks and jewelry and spices, and merchandise of every sort. Veiled women, preceded by black eunuchs, mingled with the swarthy and turbaned crowd, and shouts and cries and bargaining and chaffering resounded on every side.

Suddenly a blast of trumpets was heard from the upper extremity of the street; and every sound was immediately silenced, and all the people ranged themselves on either side, as a band of slaves dressed in green, with crooked cimeters shining in their hands, came down the way, preceding twelve officers wearing enormous turbans, mounted on black mules, and bearing brazen trumpets. When they reached the centre of the ⸱street, they stopped, and the officers sounded their trumpets and made proclamation, saying, —

"O people, listen! Thus saith the sultan, the master of the earth, the ruler of the sea, and the numberer of the stars : —

"Know, O ye people who are so blessed as to live in the city which we honor with our presence, that some child of unfathomable perdition hath stolen from our special treasury, locked with a hundred keys, guarded by a hundred slaves, entered through a labyrinth with a hundred windings, our most precious possession, the ruby ring lost in a wager to our ancestor, the great King Solomon, by the King of the Genii, and handed down ever since that day, in our most glorious and excellent house.

"Out of our great and wonderful clemency, we hereby proclaim that although he who has dared to aspire to the possession of this inestimable gem deserves a thousand deaths; yet, let him return it, and he shall receive free pardon for the offence, and shall furthermore be rewarded with two hundred purses of gold."

Then the brazen trumpets sounded again, and the slaves and the officers moved forward, and the street became more noisy than before; for all the people were wondering and lamenting over the loss from the sultan's treasury, of that wonderful ring.

But Walter of Ilzerley, as he looked around, saw one old woman, dressed as became the slave of a very rich person, who neither wondered nor questioned. She was very pale, and shook all over as she asked the merchant, by whose stall the knight had stopped his horse, whether the blue vest embroidered with gold which her mistress had ordered were finished.

"The vest is finished, and the embroidery is the finest that was ever seen in the city," answered the merchant; "but, know you, that were it not for so illustrious a lady as an inmate of the palace of our exalted master, the sultan, I should have said it had been designed for a dog of a Christian."

"What do you say?" screamed the old woman, in a shrill, quavering voice.

"Look, then," said the merchant, holding up the vest: "is not here on the breast, hidden under the waving lines of the ornaments, the outline of the unclean cross?" And he spat on the ground in sign of abhorrence. "If the lady see it, she will never wear the vest, although she sent the pattern herself."

The old woman said nothing, but paid the merchant three pieces of gold, and, taking the vest, made her way along the street as fast as she could.

The young knight followed her; but, although he took great pains not to press against any one, the crowd was so great that he constantly pushed those on the right and on the left; and they, not seeing the invisible horse and rider, felt greatly aggrieved, and angrily berated those nearest them, who, knowing themselves innocent of any discourtesy, were not slack in angry retort: and so it happened that the whole street fell into confusion, and threats and blows were exchanged on every side; and so great grew the tumult, that the merchants rose in haste and closed their shops and withdrew the awnings, and the rays of the sun poured down so fiercely that it was like a fiery rain; and so the crowd dispersed to seek shelter elsewhere; while Walter of Ilzerley followed the

old woman as she passed through many long
and winding streets. At length she halted at
a door in a high stone wall. It was the only
opening in the face of the wall, which was of
great extent.

The old woman knocked three times; and the
door was opened by a frightfully ugly slave,
whose eyes stood out so far that he looked as if
he could see all around him without turning his
head. Walter of Ilzerley sprang from his horse,
and followed the old woman as she entered;
but, although he made all the haste he could, he
did not succeed in passing the door ere the
frightful slave closed it, and the young knight
was caught between the door and the door-
post.

The slave wondered and pushed in vain, for
the door could not close, of course, since there
was a knight clothed in armor in the way. At
last the slave opened widely the door in order to
push it to with greater force, and so released the
young man, who immediately sprang forward;
but the old woman had disappeared through one
of the many doors which opened into the circular hall in which he found himself.

He had no clew to guide him in his search, so
he opened at random the door nearest him. He
saw before him a long, dark, and narrow pas-

sage, at the end of which faintly glimmered an
uncertain light. He advanced towards the ray,
which proceeded from the key-hole of a heavy
door, thickly studded with iron nails. A faint
odor of gums and spices came to his nostrils;
but he could see nothing within save by stooping to look through the key-hole, and to that no
knight could condescend. So he drew his sword
from its scabbard, and with its hilt knocked
loudly at the door. After a short delay it was
opened, and the head of an old man clothed,
although it was summer, in a furred robe, appeared. His wrinkled forehead was high and
broad; his beard was as white as snow; but his
eyebrows were black and heavy, and from beneath their shade his small, keen eyes looked
piercingly forth. As he cautiously opened the
door the young knight passed within.

The old man peered down the passage, then
muttering to himself, again closed the door.
The room, or rather vault, into which the young
knight had penetrated was vast and gloomy.
The walls were of stone whereon were deeply
graven strange devices and symbols, mixed with
Chaldean characters and Coptic signs. In the
middle of the vaulted ceiling was a small, round
aperture, through which, looking up as through
a black tube of great length, the stars could be

seen at mid-day. The air was heavy with strange perfumes, which seemed to proceed from a bronze tripod, upon which was burning a fire whose flickering and uncertain flames supplied its only light to the vault.

The old man, still muttering to himself, resumed the occupation which the knight's summons had interrupted. He took some spices and some fine powder of charcoal, and made a paste, which he moulded into the form of a ring, over which he made various signs, turning it constantly, and ever and anon turning it to the four points of the compass. Then he dropped it into the middle of the fire. Immediately a bright flame sprang up, and, detaching itself from the fire below, remained in the shape of a fiery cross, suspended in the air. When the old man saw this, he gnashed his teeth and stamped on the ground.

"What accursed mystery is this?" he exclaimed. "Three times am I foiled. And what shall I say to the sultan when he demands what I have discovered? The ring is without a doubt in Christian hands; but how it came there, it passes my science to discover." .

As he said this, the magic flame paled and died away; and, the fire on the tripod likewise sinking, the vault became dark. The old man

lighted a tall, green taper at the decaying blaze,
and placed it upon a table whereon lay a large,
black-covered book, which he began attentively
to study. Walter of Ilzerley approached, and
looked over the old man's shoulder as he bent
over the book, and he saw there written the
exact description of the ring, and an explanation
of its virtues. There he learnt that the ring had
the power, on the approach of danger, of render-
ing its possessor invisible, and knew why he
had become lost to mortal sight from the moment he approached the shore of the infidels.
He was reading with avidity the account of all
the properties of the ring which had so mysteri-
ously been bestowed upon him, when a loud
knock was heard at the iron-studded door. The
old man reluctantly arose and opened it; and
a slave, richly dressed, entered with a concerned
air, and, glancing uneasily around, knelt, and,
bending his forehead till it almost touched the
ground, said, —

"O most powerful and mighty sage! the
sultan, our master, desires. your presence forthwith."

The old man, supporting his steps with an
ivory cane carved with strange devices, followed
the messenger, who seemed in a great hurry to
get out of the vault. Walter of Ilzerley accom-

panied them through numberless passages and halls, until they came to a large room, filled with richly attired officers and slaves, who all drew aside respectfully as the old man passed. At the extremity of the room was a curtain of green brocade, before which stood ten gigantic slaves clothed in yellow, and holding naked cimeters in their hands. They made way as the old man advanced; and the slave who had summoned him drew aside the curtain, and held it up for him to enter. The knight followed close.

As he crossed the threshold, he found himself in a spacious and lofty apartment lighted with many-colored rays. The ceiling was painted to imitate the overhanging branches and green leaves of a forest, and birds of gorgeous plumage swung from it in cages of golden wire. Their songs mixed with the tinkling of a fountain which rose from a crystal tank in the middle of the room, around which grew flowers in rich abundance. Along the walls, which were of cedar inlaid with gold, were divans and cushions of embroidered damask fringed with pearl; and on the marble floor were spread carpets so soft that the footsteps falling on them gave back no sound.

On the divan at the upper end of the room sat

a young man magnificently dressed. He was handsome, though very haughty in face and bearing.

The old man knelt and touched his forehead three times to the ground as the curtain fell behind him.

"Approach, O most venerable sage!" said the sultan, "and say how your search has sped. Have you found a clew by which to track the audacious criminal who has dared to violate the sanctity of our private treasury, and to steal from it the ring?"

The sultan knit the black arches of his brows till they met, and his moustaches quivered as he spoke.

"O most glorious and gracious of sultans!" answered the old man; "something truly have I discovered, though less than I had hoped. But that which I have learned makes the loss of the ring more unaccountable than before. I know to a surety that the gem is at this moment in Christian hands."

The sultan started to his feet.

"In the hands of a dog of a Christian!" he exclaimed. "May he and his prophet perish together."

At these impious and insulting words, Walter of Ilzerley lost patience, and, drawing hastily near, he smote the sultan on the face. The blow was well planted, and it tingled sharply on the sultan's olive cheek.

" What demon, miserable old man, have you dared to bring hither with you?" he shouted in a rage, laying his hand on the dagger in his sash. " If you were less useful, your head should within five minutes make acquaintance with the bowstring. Begone! and know that unless, ere three days be over, I see again the ring, I will forget all your past services, and only remember this unheard-of affront."

So saying, the sultan, foaming with rage, clapped his hands together. The curtain was withdrawn, and the old man, half terrified to death, retreated in haste.

The sage had hardly left the room when the curtain was again lifted, and an officer, apparently of high rank, entered and prostrated himself as the old man had done.

" What news do you bring, Mustapha?" said the sultan. " Dare not to say that your quest has been unsuccessful."

" Most illustrious of sovereigns," replied the officer, " this is what I have discovered. On the night before the ring was found to be lost, some fishermen out at sea saw, in the air overhead, a bright stream of rosy light, which flashed from the direction of the city towards the country of the Christians. The night was dark, but so bright was the passing radiance that it streamed like a ruddy pathway over the water, and lighted up all the sea. Further than this, O most merciful of masters! your slave has not been able to trace the ring."

The sultan made no answer, but sat deep in thought for a while, twisting his long, curling moustache and looking on the ground. Then he made a sign to the officer to withdraw.

The sultan clapped his hands together as the officer retired, and a slave entered and prostrated himself.

"Let the great council be summoned," said the sultan; and the slave withdrew.

After a few moments the green curtain was widely withdrawn, and a procession of very old men entered. They all wore green turbans, and their white robes were girded about them by costly shawls. After the due prostrations, at a sign from the sultan they seated themselves cross-legged, folded their arms over their breasts, and waited for him to speak.

"It is known to you," said the sultan, "that our inestimable ruby ring has been audaciously stolen from our especial and private treasury."

Here all the old men bowed their heads.

" I know, from certain information, that it has passed into the unclean hands of a Christian."

Here all the old men spat on the ground, in sign of contempt and abhorrence.

" Furthermore, I have learnt that it is at this moment in the country of the Christians; and I have summoned you, to communicate to you my sovereign will and pleasure that an embassy be immediately despatched to the king of the Christians, demanding the instant return of the ring, and announcing that, should it be refused, I will ravage his country with fire and sword, and will destroy every city and walled town within its borders."

When the great councillors had heard the sultan, they all replied in chorus, —

" O most powerful and illustrious sultan! to hear is to obey."

And they left the room in the same order wherewith they had entered it; and Walter of Ilzerley joined their procession, and passed out with them.

The exterior hall looked out upon a large and shaded garden. Between the trees were seen light kiosks, whose trellised walls were wreathed with roses and jasmine; and from the velvet lawns rose numberless sparkling fountains, cooling the sultry air with their incessant rain.

Unknowing in what direction to turn in order to seek for the old woman who had bought the vest embroidered with the Christian cross, sadly perplexed at the labyrinth of halls and passages which filled the sultan's palace, the young knight passed out through an open door into the garden, and, plunging into one of the thickets of flowering shrubs, threw himself down upon the ground to consider what he was next to do.

He had not yet succeeded in arriving at any definite conclusion, when he heard footsteps coming up the broad walk which led close by him. He raised his head, and saw a hunchbacked old Egyptian female dwarf, whose contorted ugliness seemed insufferably hideous, seen as it was amidst the graceful flowers and silver fountains, and light and glory of the garden. The dwarf advanced till she was close to him; then she stopped, and said, —

" Follow me."

Walter of Ilzerley started to his feet, thinking that the ring had lost its power of concealing him ; but, as he stood upright in the sunshine, he saw that his figure cast no shadow upon the ground, and then he perceived that the dwarf must be a sorceress.

He came from the thicket and followed her through the garden, until, turning into a lonely ·

and scarcely trodden path, she stopped at a small,
carved door. She opened it by pressing upon a
spring hidden under one of its ornaments, and
passed within, followed by the knight. She
ascended a narrow and winding staircase, and
paused at a door at which she tapped. As the
door opened, the dwarf turned her head and
beckoned to the invisible knight. The door was
opened by the old woman whom he had seen
that morning bargaining for the vest. The young
man's heart leaped for joy as he saw her; and
with eager steps he passed into the room, for he
felt assured that he should find there the maiden
he sought.

The room was small, but richly decorated and
furnished in the Oriental style, with painted
arabesques, and the ceiling was carved with
curious workmanship; but the knight saw nothing save the figure of a maiden, who was whispering to herself as he entered, —

" Who shall deliver me from this captivity? "

Seated beside an open window, which looked
forth upon the sea, and leaning her cheek upon
her hand, she was steadfastly gazing upon the
glittering expanse of the water. She wore a
blue vest embroidered with gold, which half
betrayed, half concealed the graceful outlines
of her figure; her head was covered on one side

by a little embroidered cap, and on the other
was placed a bouquet of jewelled flowers; while
her long, soft, brown hair, unconfined, fell in
heavy waves almost to the ground. On her
white arms were clasped golden bracelets; and
her little, rosy feet were thrust into crimson
slippers embroidered with gold.

The knight had never seen any loveliness to
be compared with that of the maiden; and he
stood in a trance of wonder and admiration,
gazing upon her as though he would never
weary.

After a while the maiden turned from looking
over the water and spoke in a sorrowful tone to
the dwarf.

"Good mother, four days and four nights
have I watched the waves; and yet I can see no
knight coming to my rescue."

And she sighed, and, turning her head, again
fixed her eyes upon the sea.

"I can't help that," answered the dwarf,
shortly. "Some people see things where there
is nothing to be seen, and others see nothing
where there is something to be seen. I don't
make people's eyes."

And the dwarf sat down on a pile of cushions,
and sulked.

The maiden answered nothing, and did not

seem to hear the cracked and dissonant tones of the Egyptian; but the old woman who had opened the door rolled up her eyes and groaned, as if to express her disapprobation, though she evidently did not dare to speak.

As if weary of watching, the maiden left the casement, and, crossing the room, seated herself on the pile of cushions beside the dwarf. She took the old Egyptian's brown and wrinkled hand in her soft, white fingers, and said coaxingly, —

"But tell me one thing, good mother: how did you obtain for me the ruby ring? Tell me only that."

"Don't tease me," said the dwarf. "You would be sorry enough if I did tell you. The words I should be obliged to speak would shatter the walls, and bring a host of demons about us."

At these words the old woman whom the young knight had seen in the street, clasped her hands, and implored the maiden not to persist in her entreaties.

"For," said she, "know, my blessed lady, that I can scarcely sleep at nights as it is, knowing as I do that Monarè could have us all strangled by demons ere morning, if she chose. And, if I were once to see a demon, I should die

of fright outright, as, indeed, it is a wonder that
I did not that day the pirates carried us away.
But of that you knew nothing, sweet, uncon-
scious babe that you were."

And the old woman began to weep.

"Don't prate so," said the dwarf, crossly.
"Isn't it bad enough to be stolen by pirates
without being told of it all the time? Don't be
such a croaking night-owl. I wonder, for my
part, why the pirates took you. You never
could have had any good looks to boast of."

The old woman, forgetting for the moment
her fears, was about to make an angry retort,
when the maiden interfered and with gentle
words composed the menaced quarrel; then,
kissing tenderly the frightful Egyptian dwarf,
she said, —

"Good mother, how can I thank you for all
that you have done for me? If I obtain my
freedom, I will show you what my gratitude is
worth."

"Don't talk to me of gratitude," interrupted
the dwarf. "I want to know if I haven't cause
of gratitude to you. Who was it that saved me
from those Mussulman hounds in the bazaar
who were going to tear me in pieces for a witch,
only because I shortened the leg of one who was
going to kick me, so that he couldn't put it down

again? Don't talk to me of gratitude! It makes me cross."

But the maiden took no heed of the dwarf's perversity. She kept her seat by her, and caressed her cheek with her white hand.

"Well, good mother," she said, "since you will not tell me how you obtained the ring, tell me at least to whom it was that I sent it with my nightly prayer."

"A good knight and a true," answered the dwarf abruptly.

Walter of Ilzerley, at these words, could have fallen at the dwarf's feet and embraced her knees for very thankfulness, so great was his desire to stand well in the esteem of the beautiful, imprisoned maiden.

"A good knight and a true," repeated the maiden thoughtfully. "But, good mother, tell me something more. Is he young? Is he fair to look upon?"

But the dwarf would not answer a word to the maiden's questions, and only reiterated, —

"A good knight and a true."

Suddenly the maiden sprang to her feet and stood in the attitude of one listening; and the knight perceived the sound of many feet, and the clashing of arms from the garden beneath. He looked from a window that opened over the garden, and saw the old sage advancing at the head of a body of armed slaves. In his hand the old man carried a small, purple snake, which, hissing, stretched out its head in the direction of the little carved door. The old man entered, followed by the slaves, and they heard the noise of many ascending steps. The maiden stood pale and still in the middle of the room, while the old nurse crept trembling into a corner, and the dwarf clenched her teeth and stamped on the floor.

The door was wrenched open from without, and the old man appeared on the threshold. Behind him stood the slaves, filling the entry, and crowding on the stairs. The little purple snake in the sage's hand raised the crest upon its head, and hissed loudly and angrily, turning towards the window where the knight was standing.

As the dwarf caught sight of the snake, her look of rage and perplexity changed into an expression of triumph. She crept behind the maiden, whose flowing robe concealed her from view, and, crossing her hands behind her, she mumbled a few unknown words.

As she spoke them, the little snake writhed violently; then, springing from the old man's hand, it darted to the window, and disappeared.

The old man tore his hair.

" Ten purses of gold to whoever catches the snake ! " he shouted. And he and all the armed slaves rushed down the stairs in pursuit of the little purple snake ; and the sound of their voices and trampling steps died away.

The old nurse, shaking and trembling, crawled forward and closed the door; while the hideous Egyptian dwarf threw herself on the floor, and rolled her head about in an ecstasy of delight.

" Oh, what a fool, what a world-renowned fool, is that sage! Call him a sage, indeed ! Why, if I were to pull out an eyelash, that eyelash would have more knowledge in it than he has in his whole body. I want to know if he ever lived, like me, in the secret chambers of the great Pyramid, where the books of my ancestors, the Egyptian priests, are stored? What does he know, the bungler! He didn't even know who I was. And to bring that absurd little snake here where I am ! Ha, ha, ha ! "

And the dwarf rolled about and shrieked with laughter, while the old nurse looked at her aghast, and ever and anon crossed herself; and the maiden stood pressing her hand against her heart, as if to still its frightened beatings ; for, at the appearance of the armed slaves, she had anticipated nothing less than instant death.

At length the dwarf's laughter came, as all things will, to an end.

"Do stop crossing yourself," she said peevishly to the old nurse. "Can't any one have a little quiet merriment, but you must put on a long face, and scratch crosses all over yourself?"

And she turned her back upon the old woman, and, approaching the trembling maiden, took hold of her hand, and drew her to a divan.

"Sit down, my pearl, my white dove," she said caressingly. "Don't shiver so. Do you think your old Monarè would let any one hurt you? I will make that old fool repent of having frightened my child."

And she began to mutter some strange words. But the maiden laid her hand upon the Egyptian's mouth, and prayed her not to harm the sage.

"You'll make me forget all the curses I ever learned," said the dwarf, sulkily; "but if you don't want him hurt, it's all the same to me."

The maiden rose, and looked out anew upon the waves.

"Good mother, I can see nothing," she said. "When will he come?"

"That's a reasonable question," replied the dwarf, "seeing that he has been in the room for half an hour."

The blood rushed crimson into the maiden's cheeks as she glanced around.

"There's no use in looking for him," said the dwarf. "You can't see him, but I can. Young knight, don't stand there like a stone, with your eyes as wide open as if you were trying to eat her with them. Come here and kiss her hand."

But the young knight did not dare to advance towards the beautiful maiden; and she, on her side, drooped her head, and turned shyly away from that part of the room to which the dwarf directed her eyes.

"I never saw such tiresome people," said the dwarf, in a pet. "There's this young knight, as handsome as he can be, if you could only see him, come over the sea three days and three nights from the country of the Christians, because you called him; and now that he is here, you turn away and won't hold out your hand, and he is afraid to come and take it. I am angry. Hold out your hand; and you, Sir Knight, come forward."

When the maiden heard herself thus rebuked, she held out her hand, blushing all over like the sky at sunrise; and Walter of Ilzerley, advancing, fell on his knees and raised it to his lips. As she felt the invisible lips pressed upon her hand, the maiden uttered a little cry, and drew close to the dwarf's side.

" Don't be frightened," said the dwarf. " You know that you have been looking out of the window four days and four nights, hoping to see him."

At this the maiden blushed more deeply than before, and looked imploringly at the Egyptian.

" Well, well," said the dwarf, " I didn't say any thing, did I? But I must tell now this young knight what he has to do."

So saying, she turned to Walter of Ilzerley.

" As soon as it is dark the guards will make their rounds. When they appear you must attack them."

The maiden, hearing this, exclaimed, —

" O good mother! surely you do not wish the knight to fight single-handed against six ! "

Walter of Ilzerley would have assured her that he was willing to fight single-handed against sixty, for her sake ; but the same charm that rendered him invisible deprived him of the power of speech. He could but clench the handle of his sword and wish for the moment that should prove how little he valued danger in her cause.

He had not long to wait, for the night was fast coming on. It was no sooner dark than heavy steps were heard ascending the stairs; the door was thrown open, and showed the chief of the guard and his armed soldiers, each holding a lighted torch in one hand and a naked cimeter in the other. They gloomily looked around the room to assure themselves of the presence of all its inmates. At that instant Walter of Ilzerley threw from him the ring, and stood in shining armor and with flashing eyes before their astonished sight. They raised their cimeters and rushed upon him, but he sprang to meet them with uplifted sword. The quiet little room was filled with the clashing of weapons and the fierce cries of the guards; but the fray did not last long. One after another fell under the heavy blows of the Christian knight, until all six lay stretched upon the ground.

"That is well done," said the dwarf, who had watched the combat with great delight, clapping her hands and screaming with laughter as each successive guard fell to the ground; while the maiden had thrown herself upon her knees, and, burying her face in her hands, was praying earnestly; and the old nurse had crept under a pile of cushions, where nothing was visible of her save her feet.

"Now," said the dwarf, "take from the sash of the chief of the guard the key which you will find there. It opens every lock in the palace. With that we can let ourselves out."

The knight took the key from the sash of the chief of the guard, as the dwarf had directed; then taking up the ruby ring, he offered it to the maiden.

" Do as I bid you," said the dwarf, " and put it on your hand again."

The knight would have expostulated, but the Egyptian grew angry, and stretched her hand towards him, making a sign. Immediately the ruby ring slid up his finger, and he again became invisible. He tried to remove it, but it remained fast, and he had nothing to do but to submit.

Led by the dwarf, they descended the stairs, and crept stealthily along the garden. As they came near the guard-room, they heard the soldiers wondering why their chief did not return.

" I always thought harm would happen to some of us," said one of the soldiers, " ever since that Egyptian hag came into the palace. Let us go and look for them; for it grows late, and they should have been back long ago."

And, leaving the guard-room, all the soldiers came in a body into the garden, and spread themselves through it, searching for their comrades. The maiden and her attendants had crouched down in a thick clump of rose-bushes, which grew so high and broad as to quite conceal them. They remained there, until, at a loud shout, which proceeded from that part of the garden on which the little carved door opened, all the soldiers rushed thither, and they heard their cries of rage and astonishment. Then, quickly rising from their hiding-place, the maiden and the women hurried on, accompanied by the invisible knight. They passed into the deserted guard-room, and thence through many passages, until they reached the circular hall into which the knight had come on his first entrance into the palace.

"Stop here," said the Egyptian. "I must go forward and see whether the slave at the door is awake."

She stole cautiously forward, and saw the slave sitting cross-legged on the ground, his great eyes shining in the dark passage like two enormous opals. She came back grinning.

"Now I will show you something amusing," she said; and she began to draw with her finger in the air the outline of a gigantic lion. When she had finished, she blew on the air-drawn figure, and it took the form and color of life, and bounded forward with open jaws and . fiery eyes in great leaps towards the negro,

who, seeing this unexpected sight, yelled, and
took to flight, rolling with incredible agility
over and over on the floor like a ball.

The Egyptian shrieked with laughter, as the
slave, pursued by the phantom of a lion, disappeared. Then leading forward her companions,
she unlocked the little door, and they all stood
outside the palace, in the street. The knight
lifted the maiden upon his invisible horse, and,
leading it by the bridle, followed the steps of
the dwarf, who conducted them through many
dark and silent streets, down to the water's
edge.

As they neared the shore, they were startled
by a sudden glare; and, looking up, they saw
in the distance a great column of fire rising
from the watch-tower of the sultan's palace;
and the night wind brought to their ears the
sound of the clashing of arms, and loud voices.

"We must hurry," said the dwarf; "but, first,
I will make sure that we shall not be pursued."

So saying, she stooped and scraped together
a handful of sand. Then she bade them enter
a boat which lay near by.

The knight lifted the maiden from the horse,
and carried her to the boat; for, in truth, she was
so terrified that she could not have taken a step.
The old nurse hobbled in after them, casting

many an affrighted glance over her shoulder at the fast increasing, angry blaze; and the Egyptian took her place, standing in the stern; while the knight dipped the oars into the water, and rowed out to the open sea.

As the boat advanced, the dwarf let the sand fall, grain by grain, from her hand; and, as it fell, the water behind them turned to sand, and all the boats and galleys were buried fast in it, so that they could not be stirred. They saw, as they rowed away, a great crowd, led by the soldiers of the guard-room, come rushing down to the water's edge to pursue them. They heard their angry shouts and cries, and saw their unavailing efforts to raise the half-buried vessels.

The Egyptian turned as the last grain of sand fell from her hand, and, seating herself, composedly said, —

"Now we are safe. Lay down your oars, we do not need them."

A gentle wind sprang up as she spoke, the ruby ring sent forth its rosy light, and the young knight became visible. As he assumed his shape, the maiden raised her eyes timidly to his, intending to thank him; but, perceiving his look riveted upon her, she blushed, and turned away. As the knight looked upon her lovely face, and thought of the delight of her parents when they should receive the maiden from his hands, his eyes filled with tears of joy, and he almost forgot his own promised happiness in the thought of theirs.

Three days and three nights they floated over the sea, borne on by the gentle wind, which never changed nor died away, lighted by the sun by day, and by the rosy radiance of the ring at night. On the fourth night they saw a light far off on the water's edge, at the end, as it were, of the pathway traced by the ruddy rays.

When the dwarf saw the light, she heaved a deep sigh, and said to the knight, —

" Give me now the ring. You have no further. need for it."

And the knight drew from his finger the ring, and gave it to her. Then she said to the maiden, —

" Child, when you saved me from those who were about to take my life, I vowed one day to repay an equal benefit to you. Look at that light, far in the distance. It shines before your home. There, on the shore of the sea, stand your father and your mother, with out-stretched arms, waiting to embrace you. I have kept my vow. Kiss me, my child."

The maiden pressed her sweet lips to the old Egyptian's withered cheek, but suddenly she

felt upon them nothing but air. The dwarf had
vanished utterly, and the rosy light also.

"Monarè! Monarè!" cried the maiden, but
no voice replied. Only in the distance, from
the bosom of a little white cloud, came a breath
that sounded like "Farewell."

The boat sped on, wafted by the wind; and, as
it approached, they saw the light higher and
broader, and they could distinguish the figures
of the count and the countess, surrounded by all
their friends and retainers, holding high in the
air torches whose waving light flashed out upon
the sea, and showed the crowd of eager faces
all turned upon the fast advancing boat.

As the keel grated on the shore, Walter of
Ilzerley leaped from the boat, bearing the maiden,
and delivered her into her parents' arms.

They wept aloud for joy as they kissed and folded to their hearts the beautiful maiden whom they
had last seen as a babe in her nurse's arms; and
their retainers shouted for gladness in welcome
to the daughter of the house; they pressed with
joyous acclaim around the knight who had res-
cued her from the captivity wherein she had
been bound, and greeted over and over again
the old nurse who had been lost to sight for so
many years.

When her parents had kissed and blessed the

maiden, Father Anselm advanced, and laid his hand upon her head. Then the maiden and her parents, and Walter of Ilzerley, and all around, knelt upon the shore ; and the old priest lifted up his voice, and blessed the maiden, and praised and thanked God.

There was revelling at the count's castle for all that week ; and not only the rich and gay, but the poor and lonely rejoiced also, for the count and countess sent out and summoned all the poor of the whole country round, and feasted them in the court-yard, for they wished the sympathy of all in their great joy and happiness. And on the seventh day the maiden was married to the knight by Father Anselm, in the chapel of the castle, before a great crowd of lords and ladies, who had assembled from all the castles far and wide. But there was none among all the ladies who could compare for beauty and gentleness and grace with the maiden, as she stood in her long white robes and snowy veil beside the knight who had delivered her from her captivity.

APOLLYONA.

APOLLYONA.

HINK not that I was always the bowed and broken man you see me now. Though my hair is white, yet I have scarce seen thirty years. Strange and fearful is the tale I have to relate. Strange and fearful must be the penance I must still undergo ere I can merit mercy. Yet great and wonderful has been the compassion shown to me, in that I stand to-day upon the upper earth, a living man; and so I pray and dare to hope. And now will I recount the story of my sin.

Five years ago I left the lands whereof I was lord, in quest of some knightly adventure wherein to show myself a worthy servant of the saint to whose service I had vowed myself in the sore sickness from which I had but even then recovered.

I journeyed on, until, after several days, I saw in the distance a purple, white-crested wall rising high against the sky; and I knew that I saw the Pyrenees, the rocky bar that rises to shut Spain out from France. I took new courage at the sight, and pushed on my horse. The wall rose higher and higher as I advanced, breaking into numberless snowy-topped peaks. It was nightfall ere I reached the foot of the mountains, so I halted at a peasant's hut that lay half-hidden by the low spreading branches of a great oak-tree, and, knocking at the door, craved shelter for the night.

An old woman, brown and wrinkled, opened to me, and bade me welcome. She spread for my horse a provision of hay and straw, beneath the shelter of the oak; then leading me into the cottage, which was lighted by a little brass lamp, she set before me a bowl of goat's milk and a loaf of black bread.

" Once I could have offered you better cheer," she said sorrowfully, " but now this is the best I have."

While I was eating, the old woman from time to time opened the door, and gazed anxiously forth towards the mountains. She sighed heavily each time, as she returned to her seat. As I looked around the cottage, I saw on the wall the cross-bow and pouch of a hunter. I asked the old woman if she lived alone in the hut. She answered that she had one son, a hunter; but said no more. Seeing her disinclined to converse, I asked no other question. After I had finished my meal, she showed me a pallet of straw in the corner, and I lay down and fell asleep. I was soon awakened by the entrance of some one, and, opening my eyes, I saw a young man of striking form and features, though pale and haggard. He threw himself upon a stool, folded his arms on his chest, and fixed his eyes upon the ground, while the old woman placed food before him, and begged of him to eat. He took no heed of her words, and presently, rising, began to pace up and down the room, while the old woman stood with an anxious face, watching him. After a while he went to the door, opened it, and gazed forth towards the mountains. Suddenly he gave a loud cry, and exclaiming, "I see her," he sprang from the house, and sped towards the glittering peaks. The old woman burst into tears and wrung her hands, as she watched from the door his headlong course.

I rose much perplexed, and asked of her the meaning of this strange scene. She wept some time before she could answer me; at length, with many sobs, she related to me the story of the hunter, who was her only son.

He had been the bravest and most successful hunter on the Pyrenees, and was also the gayest and most light-hearted of them all. Every morning he started at sunrise alert and joyful, and returned at nightfall laden with game. But, at last, one night he did not come home. His mother sat up waiting for him all night long. The sun rose, and yet he had not returned. The next day all the hunters of the neighborhood went in search of him. They came back, bringing his cross-bow and pouch, which they had found by the side of a dead ibex, on a height covered with snow. They had tracked his footsteps higher and higher, until they led where the bravest of his comrades dared not follow. They searched for him seven days, then they gave him up as lost.

One night his old mother was sitting mourning, when the door opened and the lost hunter entered; but so pale, so changed as hardly to be recognized. He did not return his mother's caresses, nor would he answer her questions as to where he had been. He ate ravenously of the food she placed before him, then, throwing himself down, without a word, fell asleep. Early the next morning he left the hut again, and had only returned that night. His mother knew that he had seen the Witch of the Pyrenees, and that she had bewitched him.

No sooner had the old woman spoken the name of the Witch of the Pyrenees, than a longing to see her came over me; such a longing as I cannot describe. I forgot my quest, I forgot my vows as a Christian knight, I forgot my hopes of salvation. I thought of nothing save of how I might behold the Witch; and, without waiting for the sun to rise, I saddled again my horse, and, taking leave of the old woman, I pursued my way up the mountains.

At first, the path led through gently rising slopes of sod, bordered by spreading trees; but as I advanced, it became steeper and sterner, till I was obliged to dismount and make my way forward on foot. Great rocks began to rise before me, barring the path; and I heard at intervals the roar of hidden torrents, rising, as it were, from beneath my feet. I climbed with difficulty upward in the moonlight, which seemed brighter and stiller in those mountains than I had ever seen it before. I felt no fatigue; for the insatiable desire that possessed me to see the Witch

gave me strength. At length, after climbing
several hours, I came out upon an open plat-
form covered with small grass. Around, on
every side, rose bare and desolate peaks. No
living thing was to be seen. There was no
cloud in the heavens; there was no breath stir-
ring upon the earth. The silence around had
something ghost-like in it. I shivered, though I
felt no cold. Then the fever again came over
me, and I looked around, eagerly searching for
some trace of the Witch.

All at once I heard a faint, distant breath of
music. It ran through me like poison. My
limbs failed under me, and I sank on the ground,
in the shadow of a great rock, which rose on
one side of the plateau. The sweet, poisonous
voice came nearer and nearer. I heard a low
rustling rising from every side; and I saw, with
horror indescribable, glistening snakes, with
slow, writhing motion, making their way amid
the soft, green grass towards that side of the plateau to which the voice was advancing. I lay as
one paralyzed, unable to move, my eyes strained
towards the direction of the voice. Nearer and
nearer it came; at length it sounded close to me,
and I saw the figure of the Witch rise up in the
moonlight and pass on to the plateau.

My blood runs cold now, in this bright sunlight, and amid this joyous company, as I recall her form. Though hundreds of years old, she had the face and shape of a young girl, beautiful beyond the beauty of mortal woman, but with a hideous strangeness of loveliness. Her cheeks and lips were pallid as those of a corpse; her eyes shone like the death-lights that flicker over new-made graves, and her long, floating hair was white as frosted silver. In one hand she carried an ebony cup; in the other a branch, thick set with poisonous berries. Her long, white garments trailed behind her, leaving a greenish light upon the grass. A deathly chill pervaded the air as she advanced, — a chill as of a charnel-house.

Singing, followed by the snakes, she came forward, until she reached the middle of the plateau. Then she seated herself. The snakes crowded close to her, their white throats and scaly backs shining in the moonbeams as they writhed and pressed about her, uprearing their crested heads, and swaying them in motion to the song. Softly singing, she fed them with the berries, tasting the fruit herself from time to time.

As the snakes greedily closed around her, they became impatient, and grew angry with each other, hissing and darting forth their forked tongues; and one, the largest of all, suddenly turning its rage upon the Witch, reared itself from amid the writhing confusion of glistening folds, and, drawing back its head, struck at her, fastening its fangs in her white arm. The Witch laughed aloud, and patted the snake's head as the sharp teeth closed on her flesh. The laugh, clear and silvery, re-echoed again and again from the surrounding peaks. A host of demons seemed laughing in the air. A deeper chill ran over me as I listened, and yet I would not have moved to fly if I could have done so. Her beauty filled my senses to overflowing with delight; and the very horror she inspired increased her charm.

When the Witch had fed the snakes, she smoothed and caressed the head of each, singing to it a low, whispering song; and the snakes opened their mouths, and let fall from their fangs drops of poison into the ebony cup. When each snake had paid its deathful tribute, she rose and waved her hand, and all the serpents, glittering like silver lines across the grass, withdrew to their hiding-places.

As they disappeared, the Witch looked around. Her eyes rested upon me as I lay in my armor in the shadow of the rock. She drew in her breath eagerly. Her eyes grew larger, and shot

forth blazing light for an instant, then, veiling
them with her long lashes, she stole towards
me, gliding like a ripple over the sea.

She stood before me, and gazed upon me
steadfastly, with a smile upon her lips. She
bent over me, and said softly, —

"Good knight, it is cold and lonely on the
mountain-top. Will you not come with me?"

As she spoke, she laid her hand upon mine;
— and my soul fled from me, and left me a prey
to the Witch; and I rose and followed her. Led
by the Witch, I descended. Where the way had
been rough and steep, it was now carpeted with
moss, and fringed with blossoms; but beneath
every flower crouched some toad, or centipede,
or noxious creature, whose eyes shone out on
me with an exulting glare as I passed. But
when I looked on the beautiful face of the Witch,
I thought no more of them; and so she led me
through flowery paths, until we reached the
mouth of a great cavern, which opened at the
foot of a steep precipice of gray rock. The
Witch entered first, then turning, held out her
hand and smiled, and bade me follow. I sprang
forward to seize her hand. As I crossed the
threshold I heard a mighty rush behind me,
and, looking back, I saw that a cataract was
pouring from the rock overhead so as to close

the entrance of the cave. But I cared not, so long as I was not divided from the Witch.

She smiled more sweetly than before, as the torrent poured down, and bade me welcome, saying that she had long waited for me, and that all was ready for my coming. I was about to answer her, when suddenly I perceived that she had vanished. But as I was sure that she would soon return, I was not disquieted, but began to look around me, and to marvel at the wonders of the place. The floor was paved with small pebbles of different colors, so arranged as to form a mosaic of inextricable pattern; the walls were curtained with tapestry, woven of fine, green grass and flowers, corniced and fringed with rows of glow-worms, whose brilliancy shed a soft, intermittent light around.

Broad and soft divans, covered with a web of delicately shaded feathers, surrounded the cave, and invited me to rest. I sank down, and waited for the Witch's reappearance.

As I waited and listened, I thought that I heard from a distance a faint cry, as of one in pain. I sprang to my feet, fearing that harm had come to the Witch, for I thought only of her. I looked around for the way whereby she had passed out, but I could see no break in the continuous tapestry of green and flowers. While

I was wandering up and down, seeking to follow her, the hangings parted just before me, and the Witch appeared. I sprang towards her, saying, —

"I heard a cry as of one in pain, and I feared that harm had befallen you."

She answered, —

"Can you fancy that harm could befall any one in this cave of delights?"

And she laughed as she spoke. The laugh re-echoed from the softly lit cave as it had done before from the rugged mountain peaks. Again a host of demons seemed laughing in the air, and again I shuddered.

The Witch held in her hand a crystal goblet, filled with a golden liquid. She held it out to me, and bade me drink. As I took it, the glow-worms sent out more brilliant light, the grass grew greener, the flowers deeper, and the pebbles on the floor shone bright. But, as I raised it to my lips, an invisible hand struck the goblet from my hold. It shivered as it fell, and the liquid ran along the floor, leaving a mark as though lightning had passed there. I looked at the Witch, but her face was smiling and gentle as before.

"Had you thirsted, you would have held the goblet more firmly," she said. "Let me give you to eat."

And she took from her bosom a purple fruit, shaped like a heart, and bade me eat. But ere I could taste of it, it was dashed to the ground. It burst into a flame, blazed for an instant, then went out, leaving a few black ashes.

"Neither are you hungry," said the Witch; "but you are tired, and must sleep."

So saying, she took me by the hand, and, leading me to a divan, seated herself by my side. As I sank back, I raised the hand I held to my lips; but ere I had pressed them to it, I saw a drop of blood upon her wrist.

"I have scratched myself with a thorn," said the Witch, and she wiped away the blood; but there was no sign of a scratch beneath to be seen on her blue-veined wrist.

She fixed her gleaming eyes steadily upon me, moving her lips in a strange, low rhyme of words that I could not understand. Then I can remember little, save that a drowsiness stole over me, and that through it, as through a cloud, I saw the eyes of the Witch shining upon me; and I heard her voice fainter and fainter, as she murmured the rhyme of strange words over me.

When I awoke, I found myself extended on a pile of cushions. My armor had been removed, and I was arrayed in a loose silken robe. Around me stood four open censers, filled with aromatic spices and with scented woods. The flame which rose from them shed a changeful light around, dimly and by snatches revealing the rocky walls and fantastic furnishing of the chamber.

The seats were of the knotted roots of trees, each imaging some horrible and repulsive creature. On one side an anaconda rolled itself in sinuous folds around a rabbit, whose jaws were strained asunder by its death agony ; opposite, a polypus was drawing into its loathsome mouth a struggling ape, which tossed its arms wildly above its head ; here, a leopard, lithe and sinewy, pounced upon a cowering antelope ; and a little further, the thick-necked hyena revelled upon some ghastly relic torn up from a grave.

My observations were interrupted by the sound of a low chant rising from below. I started up and·listened. Women's voices were singing a slow, mournful measure : —

> " I saw a star fall,
>   In my dream;
>   It shot down headlong,
>   With a gleam
>   Of fading light,
>   Into the night, —
>   Lost, lost, for ever lost."

The voices paused ; then again repeated, in

tones that were like the distant moaning of the pines, —

"Lost, lost, for ever lost."

There was something in the warning accent of the song that disquieted me. The fumes of the burning essences, which had hitherto soothed me into a state of half-unconsciousness, all at once cleared away from my senses. I arose, and looked around over the floor. I saw a crevice whence came a faint glimmer of light. I knelt and looked through the aperture. Below was a vast, dimly lighted hall. In its centre was a great loom, around which was standing a group of maidens. To my horror, I perceived that each of them wore a serpent as a girdle; the serpents' heads were turned upward, and rested upon each maiden's breast.

On the loom was a web of strange design. It shimmered and glanced as though jewels had been melted for the dyes. I had scarcely time to snatch one look at the band of serpent-girdled maidens, when all the serpents raised their heads, and, angrily hissing, menaced the damsels, with uplifted crests and widely gaping jaws. Thereat the maidens began hurriedly to weave the web, and sang no more.

When the snakes heard the sound of the loom

they again couched their heads upon the maidens' bosoms, and seemed to sleep.

After they had worked for some time in silence, I felt a sudden throb in all my pulses, and saw the figure of the Witch gliding forward from one of the darker recesses of the hall. The maidens did not raise their eyes as she approached, but I saw them shiver as with cold.

The Witch came near and examined the web.

"It is soft as a dead child's hair," she said; "as firm as a drowned man's grip."

She turned away.

"Bring me my robe made from the veil of the great temple," she said, "and the ornaments that Astarte wore of old."

The maidens disappeared, and presently returned, bearing a garment of blue and purple and scarlet, embroidered with such richness that I had never seen the like. And they attired the Witch in the robe; and they placed upon her long white hair a coronet of golden towers, and around her neck and arms they clasped the wondrous ornaments that Astarte wore of old.

When she was thus arrayed, she was so marvellously beautiful that my heart stopped beating, and I felt the blood rushing in my ears. I staggered back, and fell upon the cushions; one consciousness alone left me, — the remembrance of the beauty of the Witch.

As I lay, a curtain was drawn aside, and the maidens I had seen entered in procession, each bearing a lighted torch. They formed themselves into two rows, holding aloft the torches they carried; and then I beheld the Witch gliding towards me in her royal, rainbow robes, the greenish light trailing from her footsteps.

She approached and took my hand, and said softly, —

"Arise, my guest, and deign to sup with me."

And I arose, and the Witch led me forth into a great, glittering hall. On every side I saw the transparent sheen of falling water, but all was still, — there was no sound save the low murmur of the Witch's voice as she spoke to me. The hall was illumined with a silvery light that shone through the surrounding cascades. The floor was covered with fine white sand. In the midst stood a table made of an enormous seashell. On it were piled luscious viands and sparkling wines.

The Witch placed me at the table, and seated herself beside me. With her dainty fingers she presented me with food, and poured sparkling wine into the goblet that stood near me.

At first I had thought the Witch and myself

were the only beings within the hall; but, as I looked more attentively around, I began to perceive strange and monstrous forms behind the encircling sheet of falling waters. They gibbered and mocked at me as I glanced from side to side, their transparent outlines appearing and disappearing in the ceaseless motion of the cascades; and writhed and contorted themselves in silent ecstasies of demoniac glee.

"What are those forms that gaze, mopping and mowing upon me?" I said to the Witch.

And she replied, —

"Nay, mine honored guest, your eyes are dazzled by the light that plays along the water, — ye behold nought else."

And, looking upon her as she spoke, I forgot again to glance upon the moving waters with their unearthly forms. I ate and drank, and the Witch watched me with gleaming eyes.

When I ceased eating, —

"Come," said the Witch, who had tasted nothing, "let us sit and talk awhile together."

And she led me to the upper end of the hall, where I perceived a divan beneath a canopy. Yet I was sure that it had not been there when I entered.

As she placed herself beside me, the rainbow folds of her dress fell so close that they rested

6

on me. I looked down upon the rich embroidery, and wondered whether I had heard rightly, and whether it were indeed the veil of the great temple.

"How beautiful is the robe!" I said to the Witch. And she answered, smiling, —

"It comes from far. Shall I tell you its history?"

And I prayed her to speak on.

"When Titus had banded his legions around Jerusalem, so that no one could enter or go out of the city; and when the Jews were so pressed by hunger that they had no longer even leather or parchment to devour, and mothers ate their children, and men opened their veins and drank of their own blood; then some of the priests of the temple said to each other, —

"'Jehovah has deserted us. Let us call upon the Demons. Perchance they may hear and save us, even now.'

"And at midnight they met in the inner court of the temple. The night was dark and wild. The wind howled along the crests of the barren mounts around, and brought to their ears the distant cries of the Roman guards, as they relieved each other. The watch-fires of the beleaguering hosts glimmered in a circle all around the city, telling how close the besiegers had come, and revealing the artisans, busy on the great catapults and battering-rams and movable towers, by the aid of which the city was to be stormed on the morrow. All was motion and preparation in the camp without; while within, the wailing of the imprisoned Jews, and the despairing moan of women and children, rose from the city below, to the mount of the temple.

"The priests built a fire of cedar wood, such as the Demons love, in the middle of the court; and around it they traced the magic circle, and the forbidden signs. Then each priest cut a lock of hair from the right side of his head, and cast it into the blaze, repeating the invocation to the Demons of the Air. But the Demons of the Air were deaf to their call, and would not answer. Then they sacrificed anew, each throwing a lock of hair cut from the left side of the head upon the pile, and they repeated the invocation to the Demons of the Earth. And the ground shook and opened before their feet, and they saw a flight of shadowy steps. They were hastening towards them, when they heard a sound like distant thunder, saying, —

" 'Come not with empty hands into the kingdom below.'

" So each priest, with fear and trembling, laid

his hands upon such of the treasures of the temple as stood nearest; and one of them tore down the veil of the tabernacle, and bore it away. Long years it remained hidden among the treasures of the Demons of the Earth, until, in recompense for a service I had rendered them, they bade me choose from their treasury that which I most coveted, and I took the veil."

I was filled with astonishment as the Witch spoke. Seeing my wonder, she asked me if I wished to behold all the marvels contained in the treasury of the Demons. I had no sooner answered, than she laid one hand upon my shoulder, and placed the other over my eyes; then she whispered some words that I could not understand, and suddenly I felt myself uplifted and borne through the air, the Witch's hand still over my eyes, the other still resting on my shoulder. A long time seemed to elapse, and still I felt the quick rush of the air upon me. At times it was cold as ice; at others, we would pass through heated blasts that scorched me, and again we would float through soft, scented air, such as I never breathed on earth. At length I rested on my feet, and the Witch removed her hand from my eyes.

I found myself in a hall of incalculable extent, lined with polished steel. Around, on pedestals

of porphyry, stood colossal statues of iron, each
with fiery eyes. The shining steel around reflected these myriad fires, and diffused a blinding light. I veiled my dazzled eyes with my
hands, but so intense was the glare about me
that the bone and muscle seemed but as a ruddy
veil before my sight. Gradually I became accustomed to the brilliancy, and was able to look
about me. On every side I saw piles of gems
and of precious metals ; but these were the least
of the wonders of the place. The Witch showed
me, preserved there, the curious works and cunning inventions of mighty races whose very names
are forgotten, whose cities lie buried hundreds
of feet below the ice of the poles, where the
earth, she said, first grew cool enough for man
to live thereon ; and, as she showed them, she
told me of the wars they waged against the
Demons of Fire ere they could dispossess them,
and of the centuries of their increasing empire,
until, at length, they met and fought till they
destroyed each other, and their memory per-
ished from off the earth. And she displayed
to me the crowns and sceptres of all the mon-
archs who have ever ruled over mankind ; for, at
the death of each, the Demons steal their royal
insignia, and replace them with others fabri-
cated in the depths below. And so I beheld all

the history of the world written in diadems;
and I marvelled to see how small a thing is
earthly state, and how fleeting are man's most
hoarded possessions. And I saw also the magic
wands of all the sorcerers. The vipers still
twined, living, about that of Aaron; but around
the others were but dried and faded skins.
And the Goblet of Dreams was there, with ever
shifting sides of uncertain hues, and the Cap
of Soothsaying and the Sandals of Speed. A
lifetime would not suffice me were I to attempt
to recount all the wonders I looked upon: the
shell of the tortoise, from whose withered sinews
still breathed a low, harmonious plaint; the
girdle of Masinta, with which she snared the
kings; the cup whence the draught of hemlock
poured death through godlike veins; the hau-
berk of the hero who led the Scandinavian hosts
into the halls of victory: — I cannot recount the
thousandth part of what I gazed upon. But one
thing more than aught else drew my attention.
It was a small, black vial, from whose mouth
a violet cloud curled ceaselessly upward. I
questioned the Witch concerning it.

" It is nothing," she answered quickly, " nothing;" and she sought to draw me away. I
yielded, and she led me on through wonders
without ceasing. As long as I heard her sweet,

whispering voice, I remembered no more the
vial; but at every pause the thought of it returned upon me, and I wondered what it could
contain, and why she so anxiously sought to
draw me from it. I determined, at length, to
obtain possession of it, if possible.

The Witch still seemed uneasy.

"Come with me into the gardens of the
Demons," she said, as if she suspected my secret
resolve.

She led me up some steps, to a sculptured
golden door which she unclosed, and we passed
out into gardens of wondrous beauty, inter-
spersed with thickets of flowering shrubs, and
groves of lofty trees. But every thing wore a
strange and ghost-like look. The light was reflected upwards from the ground, which was
formed of gold dust. Above, instead of the
blue sky, was a black vault, void of sun or moon
or stars. No cloud floated over it. It was like
the darkness ere the earth had being. No
breeze waved the trees around; their boughs
and shining leaves stood motionless; the gorgeous flowers on every hand gave forth no
perfume; no blade of grass stirred as we
moved on.

The Witch led me over the green lawns towards a fountain. I stooped to dip my hand in

it, but drew back astonished. No water had met my touch, — it was a sheet of polished and fretted crystal. I turned aside to pluck a flower. Its stem resisted my effort; it was hard as iron; and, looking more closely, I saw that it was an enamelled counterfeit. " The birds, at least, are real," I said to myself; and just then one sailed slowly down and lighted near me. I laid my hand upon it to caress it. Its feathers were cold and unyielding, and I perceived that it was a curiously constructed machine.

" See how much nobler are these than the perishing delights of earth," said the Witch. " No storms bring desolation to this land; no fierce winds shiver the adamantine trees; no worm destroys these shrubs; no blight withers these blossoms, nor does the envious night conceal the beauties around. The trivial and ceaseless change of hours and seasons is unknown here. Such as you see them, these gardens have existed ages before the flood."

" But where are the Demons?" I questioned, looking around, for I saw no one.

The Witch laughed mockingly.

" Where?" she rejoined. " Answer, O Demons, where are ye?"

And a deafening chorus of voices, above, below, on every side, replied, —

" Here are we, here ! "

So threatening was the sound, that I started, and laid my hand instinctively upon my dagger.

At the gesture a peal of such demoniac laughter arose that I dropped the weapon, and sought to close my ears. After a while I removed my hands. A dead silence was around me. I heard only the singing of the unreal birds.

I felt myself unable to endure the presence of the crowd of unseen beings, and I said to the Witch, —

" Show me, I beg you, the Demons who fill these gardens."

She looked at me with a strange smile.

" They are not beautiful to look upon," she replied.

Nevertheless, I persisted in my entreaty.

" You do not know what you ask," she said. " You will not dare to pass through the fiery veil."

But still I insisted, and the Witch no longer said me nay.

" We must obtain permission of the King," she said ; " but he is my friend of old, and will refuse me nothing."

She led me across many broad and glittering terraces, until at length we paused before a wall of solid rock. It was so vast that its summit lost itself in the darkness above, nor could my eye measure the extent of its surface on either side. In its centre was an enormous portal of some metal unknown to me, curiously banded, and fastened with massive chains.

The Witch tapped gently. At the summons the chains fell, the bars unclosed, and the giant gates swung backward with a jarring clash.

A vast, black hall appeared before us, lighted with pyramids of fire, which flamed in rows on either side. At the upper extremity of the hall was a mighty throne, which blazed so fiercely that I could not raise my eyes to it. I could see no living form in the hall.

The Witch led me towards the throne, stretched forth her hand, and said, —

"O most powerful enemy of God, thou who dost unsubdued maintain thy sway over hosts of those whom he calls his children! great Mammon, hear and grant my prayer. Let this child of earth behold thee and thy subjects as ye are."

A deep and awful voice answered, —

"He has not passed through the probation."

And the Witch made reply, —

"Truly, great Mammon, I ask a hitherto ungranted boon; but I hold dear the desires of this child of man, and therefore again I beseech thee to fulfil this my request."

" So be it !" said the awful voice. And thereupon I heard a crash as though the foundations of the earth were being loosed, and a blinding curtain of flame wrapped itself around me, so that I lost all consciousness of where I was, and deemed myself drowning in a fiery sea. Then the reverberations ceased, the curtain of flame was withdrawn, and, raising my bewildered eyes, I saw, seated on the dazzling throne, a terrific shadow of gigantic size. Its port was regal beyond the majesty of earth ; it held a shadowy sceptre in its cloudy hand, and on its blackened brow it wore a diadem. But, gazing steadily upon it, I saw through its breast; and, where there should have been a heart, there was a stone.

Horror-stricken, I averted my eyes ; and, lo, the hall was full of shadows, and all in their bosoms carried stones for hearts. Some of the shadows wore the mien of weighty magistrates ; some had the martial bearing of the leaders of armies ; some presented the semblance of holy priests. Students, wan and wasted, were there ; princes and magnates also. Nor were the crowd composed of the shadows of men alone. I saw there women, some old and haggard, stooping with weight of years; some young and fair, with rounded forms and graceful outlines: but all alike bore in their bosoms a stone instead of a heart.

And I shrank and shuddered, and said to the Witch, —

" Lead me away."

But she smiled in mockery, and replied, —

" Nay, have you not your wish?"

And I implored still more earnestly that she would lead me away; for I feared in my own thoughts that, did I longer tarry, my heart, also, would turn into a stone.

And the Witch made obeisance to Mammon, and we turned away.

She conducted me through spacious banqueting-rooms, lined and paved with marbles from the inner chambers of the earth, of brilliancy such as I had never seen before.

"When mortals seek for these stones, they find only what Nature has cast aside as failures," said the Witch. " The Demons only have access to the secret recesses where she stores her precious things."

We passed on through sumptuous courts and gleaming galleries, until my brain ached with the incessant glare; for all were lighted from the ground, which gave a ghastly and unreal aspect to every object that I beheld. Moreover, I still shrank and shuddered at the presence of the silent, shadowy throngs which filled the palace.

The Witch remarked my uneasiness.

"Come," she said, in her sweet, whispering voice, "let us return into the gardens, and repose ourselves under the adamantine trees."

And again I gave up my soul to her as a bird yields itself up to the fowler; and she led me through golden gates into the glittering gardens. But here, also, were the shadows. I closed my eyes not to see them ; and, turning to the Witch, I prayed that she would take from me the newly bestowed gift of sight.

She breathed three times upon my eyelids, and, when I again opened my eyes, I saw no more the shadows with their hearts of stone : I beheld only the face of the Witch shining upon me.

We seated ourselves beneath the adamantine trees, and the Witch began to tell me a tale in a voice so sweet that I could have listened to her for ever.

"When Sardanapalus was king of the East, and his power was so great that no other prince's name was spoken in all the earth save his, he went out one day with a mighty train to hunt. He took his way towards the hills, to the north

of the city, where a wild boar, of enormous size
and great fierceness, had made its appearance,
and was devastating all around. The dogs
sought for it long in vain, at the place where it
had last been seen; at length, in .a deep fell,
they found it, and forthwith gave it chase. The
creature was swift and wily, and led the king
and his train very far away. At last, rising
beyond a barren plain, they saw a high mountain. Its peaks were bare and scorched; no
grass or trees grew on its arid sides; no birds
sailed over it; the sunlight, bright on all beside,
refused to touch it; a dark shadow veiled it,
although there were no clouds in the sky. The
boar, which still seemed as fresh as when the
dogs first roused it from its lair, took its un-
wieldy way across the plain, and hid itself in
the recesses of the dark mountain.

"When the king's attendants saw where the
animal had taken refuge, they all drew their
bridle-reins, and besought him to go no farther.
But the king scoffed at their importunity, and
bade them go on. Then an old man, who had
been the king's governor in his youth, told him
that a prophecy was written in the most ancient
of the sacred books, that, should the king once
set his foot upon that mountain, the kingdom
would be destroyed.

" But the king jeered at him, and bade all his traîn rejoin the hounds, who were barking shrilly and loudly, having brought the boar to bay. And he set spurs to his horse, and forced him up the mountain side, and all the courtiers followed him.

" When they reached the defile wherein the boar had been brought to bay, they found the dogs in a sore plight: some tossed here and there, dying; the rest mangled, bleeding, fearing to approach more closely, encircled, baying furiously, the monster, who stood, his coarse mane bristling, his small, red eyes glowing, the white foam flying from his jaws as he gnashed his frightful tusks and glared around. The king ordered a second pack of hounds to be unleashed; but just as they were dashing boldly forward upon their foe, and Sardanapalus was eagerly bending from his saddle to view the strife, — for he delighted in such contests, and the longer and the fiercer they were the better he was pleased, — a strange dog, of wonderful size and beauty, sprang down the rocks, and seized the boar by the throat with so close a grip that he laid him dead on the ground.

" The king turned white with rage at this bold intrusion and the speedy close to which it had brought his sport, and he forthwith ordered one of the slaves to slay the dog on the spot. The slave went forward to where the hound stood proudly over the prostrate monster, and, drawing his short, two-edged sword, stabbed him to the heart.

" As the dog's dying howl rang out, a cry of grief sounded from above; and, looking up, they saw on an overhanging point of rock the figure of an old man. They had scarcely time to glance upward ere he was gone; and though the king ordered search to be made for him, he could not be found; and Sardanapalus, in a sullen mood at the loss of the chief pleasure of the day, turned back towards the city, while his attendants rode with downcast heads, pondering on the rashness of the king, and on its probable evil consequences.

" A week passed by, and nothing unusual occurred. Day by day, with unfailing punctuality, the wonted messengers arrived from the different provinces which owned the sway of Sardanapalus, and all brought the accustomed tidings of peace and prosperity everywhere. The sun shone bright, the heavens were without a cloud, and the doomed king looked around him and laughed in his heart the prophecy to scorn.

" At noon, on the eighth day, the guards on the palace wall saw a mighty crowd approaching, following an old man, who led a black horse by the · bridle. The confused cries and shouts of wonder and astonishment of the people filled the air, and reached even to the inner chambers of the palace where the king sat. As the old man drew nearer, the guards perceived that the horse's daintily-stepping hoofs were of gold, and that its flowing tail, and the ample mane which it tossed impatiently from side to side, were of shining silver.

" When the old man, leading the horse, had reached the great gate of the palace, he made obeisance to the captain of the guard, and humbly craved an audience of the king.

" And Sardanapalus, surrounded by those who were with him, came out upon a balcony above the great court, and ordered the old man and the wonderful horse to be brought before him.

" The old man prostrated himself, and said, —

" ' O most powerful king ! deign to look graciously upon thy servant, and to accept the gift he brings : a horse from the plains which crown the Mountains of the Moon.'

" And the king, with courteous words, accepted the gift, and ordered as much gold as three horses could carry to be given to the old man.

" As the stranger rose from the ground, he

7

glanced for an instant upward at Sardanapalus;
and all those who stood around him on the balcony closed their eyes involuntarily, as at a bolt
of lightning; and even the king shrank back an
instant, as does a sleeper before whose closed
eyelids the light of a lamp is flashed.

"The king's governor, who stood behind him,
bent forward and looked earnestly at the retreat-
ing figure of the old man, who, conducted by the
slaves of the court, was leading the horse towards
the king's stables; and said, —

"'O king! unless my eyes deceive me, I behold again the old man who stood on the peak
of the Fatal Mountain, when the strange hound
was slain. I beseech you, O king! send away
the horse and its giver. I foresee that no good
will come of the gift.'

"But Sardanapalus, who loved a noble steed,
and cared for no pleasure save the manly one of
the chase, paid no heed to his governor's words,
and began to congratulate himself on his good
fortune in becoming the possessor of such an
unequalled barb. While he was still expressing
his satisfaction, the captain of the guard of the
stables entered, with a troubled face, and related
that when he had conducted the old man to the
stable of marble, for that he had judged the horse
worthy of that place of honor, the stranger had

requested to lead in the steed alone. They had waited long for him to come out, and had at length followed him within. The horse was there fastened by the bridle, but the old man had vanished.

" The king knit his brows.

" ' What! does the old man despise my gift?' he exclaimed. 'Seek him throughout the city, and bring him before me that he may name his own reward. It shall never be said that Sardanapalus was a niggardly giver; sooner shall he have a province for the horse.'

" Then again the governor, still more alarmed at the old man's disappearance than before, implored the king to send away the horse; but Sardanapalus rebuked him sharply, and ordered the master of the hunt to have all in readiness to start at daybreak the next morning. Having done this, he proceeded, followed by his great officers, to the council chamber, and there listened to the reports sent in from his different provinces, and transacted all affairs of state for that day and the next; for he was a wise and prudent ruler, and prized the welfare of his people above all else.

" The morrow broke fair and cloudless. A cool, inviting breeze tempered the heat, and waved the branches of the trees upon the hanging gar-

dens which surrounded the palace. As the sun
rose redly over the eastern hills, the trumpets
sounded in the outer court; and the king with all
his officers and attendants, arrayed in hunting
garb, came forth from the inner apartments.
The horses stood ready for them. The black
barb, superbly caparisoned, awaited its rider.
It stood quiet and unmoved; but all the other
horses seemed wild with affright. They were
backing and rearing, their eyes starting, their
nostrils distended, and the sweat pouring from
their haunches. The slaves could with difficulty
restrain them.

" 'What is this?' said Sardanapalus, laughing
as he saw the scene of confusion. 'Is there a
lion in the court?'

"And he patted the neck of the black steed,
with its mane of shining silver, and vaulted into
the saddle. As he settled himself firmly in his
seat, the horse turned its head over its shoulder
and looked at him. The same bolt of lightning
that they had an instant seen on the day before,
again blinded the eyes of all around; and again
the king shrank, as does a sleeper before whose
closed eyelids a sudden light is flashed.

"They left the city and careered gayly across the
plain, until at length they reached the open coun-.
try. Ere long the brisk cry of the dogs and the

cheery calls of the slaves gave notice that the
game was scented. At that instant the black
barb made a furious bound, and darted away
with incredible swiftness. In vain the king used
every art of horsemanship to check its speed.
It spurned at them all, and still flew onward
like the wind. For a while Sardanapalus heard
behind him his attendants, as they sought in vain
to rejoin him; but gradually the sound of their
cries and the trampling of their horses' hoofs
died away, and he was in the wilderness alone,
still borne onward as by the sweep of a mighty
wind.

" The horse stayed not its course by field nor
by flood, till at last the king saw, rising across
the barren plain, the dark outline of the Fatal
Mountain. Again, as the prophecy rushed upon
his memory, he strove, with straining nerve and
swelling muscle, to check the headlong course
of his steed, and again he found his every effort
powerless. As they neared the mount, the horse
raised its head and neighed. The sound rever-
berated like thunder from the scathed and riven
peaks, and lost itself in hollow mutterings among
their obscure recesses.

" The horse sprang up a rugged and stony defile,
and, winding its way with unabated speed through
a series of labyrinthine turnings, finally bore its

rider into a deep and narrow gorge. Scowling rocks rose on either side till they seemed to touch the sky. A sulphurous stench filled the air, so that the king could scarcely draw his breath. No trace of life, not even an insect nor a tuft of moss, was to be seen. It seemed the very home of desolation.

"The steed dashed over the masses of broken rock which obstructed the valley. Darkness began to close about Sardanapalus as he was borne forward. It gathered fast, until, when the horse finally halted, he could distinguish nothing.

"The king's first impulse was to throw himself from the back of the golden-footed horse; his next, to gaze, giddy, bewildered, and perplexed, through the darkness around. He saw a faint light gleaming from the all but inaccessible mouth of a cave above him. As it caught his eye, an irrepressible fever of curiosity seized upon him. He clambered with difficulty, groping his way, up the rocky face of the precipice, and stood at the entrance of the grotto. An unexpected sight met his eye.

"Beside a crystal lamp, on a low stool, sat a Woman spinning. Her robe, which fitted closely to her form, was of scarlet; her long hair, unbound, caught the light and shone like fire. Her eyes were cast down upon her work; and she was singing a sweet, strange rhyme.

"As Sardanapalus looked upon the Woman, the remembrance of his wild ride, of the Fatal Mountain, and of the ancient prophecy in the sacred book, faded from his memory as a wreath of morning mist disappears before the noontide heat. He would have drawn near and spoken to her; but an awe, hitherto unknown to him, fettered his limbs and chained his tongue. He stood motionless, gazing on her" —

"As I on you," broke from my lips.

And the Witch smiled, and her eyes gleamed, and she repeated, —

"Yes, as you on me."

"The Woman span, still singing her sweet, strange song, until the wool on the spindle was ended. Then she arose from her seat beside the crystal lamp, and, moving towards the king, she said, without raising her eyes, —

"'O stranger, speak! wherein can I serve you?'

"But Sardanapalus was so amazed at her beauty that he answered her never a word.

"Then she took him by the hand and led him gently forward, and placed him on the seat whence she had risen. And she set before him vessels of gold and of silver, and she served him with meat and wine. Then she made him to

recline upon a couch of cushions ; and she again
began to spin, singing the while her rhyme.

"And, as Sardanapalus listened, his strength
melted as wax before the fire, and his manhood
fell away from him like a garment that is cast
aside ; he forgot his kingdom and his people, his
honor, his glory, and all that he had hitherto
loved and delighted in ; and, as the fool's soul left
him, he closed his beclouded eyes, and tears of
soft pleasure rolled down his sunburnt cheeks,
and rested on his manly beard." And again the
Witch laughed as I before had heard her, and
again the mocking fiends seemed laughing in the
air.

"When the lords and attendants saw their king
borne away by the black steed, they tore their
hair, and roused the echoes with their lamentations. They knew not which way to seek the
monarch, nor dared they return to the city without him.

"Then the old governor spoke. His words
were few. He said, —

"'To the Fatal Mountain ! There shall we
find the king.'

"And the train, suddenly struck into silence,
obeyed.

"Long they sought Sardanapalus in vain among
the riven peaks and blasted recesses and ravines

and shadows of the mountain. At length the old governor, with a few others, made his way through the tortuous defile into the darkness of the valley ; and there, on the face of the precipice, they saw the glimmering of light from the mouth of the grot. They climbed the rock and entered. They saw the Woman in her scarlet robe, sitting by the lamp of crystal, spinning and softly singing ; and on the couch beyond lay Sardanapalus, asleep.

"'Accursed one!' said the governor to the woman, 'by what devilish arts hast thou ensnared our king?'

"And she answered, smiling gently, 'Nay, my lord, I knew not that it was the king. A stranger, weary and fasting, sought refuge here, and I gave him food and rest. Did I not well?'

"But the old governor hearkened not to her words. He stood by Sardanapalus, and implored of him to rise. Then the king sat up, and looked with a vacant and irresolute air around upon his servants.

"'Hasten hence, O king! I beseech you. It is evil for you to be here,' prayed the governor.

"But the king paid no heed. He still gazed vacantly around, until his eyes rested on the

Woman. Then a sudden light broke from them.
He arose and drew near her. And the Woman,
with fair words and downcast eyes, bade him
farewell. The king cast himself on the ground
at her feet, and prayed of her that she would
come with him. And the governor and those
who were with him grew crimson with shame
to see the degradation of so mighty a monarch ;
but the Woman was in no wise moved by his
entreaties, and obstinately refused to leave the
cave. Then the king rose furiously to his feet,
and ordered his attendants to seize upon her and
bear her away. The governor would have again
spoken, but Sardanapalus, foaming with rage,
cursed at him with a fearful oath, and bade him
hold his peace for a dotard ; and again he commanded his courtiers to lay hold upon the
Woman and bear her away. And they raised
her in their arms and bore her from the cave ;
but, as they moved forward, they gazed at each
other in affright. ·No weight rested on their
arms. They seemed to be bearing a vision
away.

   " Warily they descended the precipice. When
they had reached the ground, according to the
king's command, they sought for the black horse ;
but it was gone, and no one ever beheld it more.

   " They made their way with difficulty over the

rough and jagged rocks, the king holding himself ever beside the Woman, as she was borne forward in the courtiers' arms. As they neared the exit from the labyrinthine windings of the valley, they saw above them, sharply defined against the impending shadow, the figure of the old man. But, as they gazed, it vanished into thin air, cheating their sight. They were terrified, and pressed forward more rapidly, casting anxious glances over their shoulders; but Sardanapalus had seen nothing, his eyes were fixed upon the face of the Woman.

"They halted as they emerged from the shadow of the mountain; and the king with many entreaties implored the Woman to forgive him for having brought her away by force, and besought her thenceforth to accompany him willingly. And she answered him, saying that, since resistance would be vain, she must perforce submit. But, although her words were discourteous, they delighted the king, who trusted to propitiate her later.

"He caused her to be mounted upon a white horse, and he rode on by her side, bending from his saddle-bow to catch each accent of her low, whispering voice; and so they proceeded slowly on, until at even-tide they entered the city and gained the palace.

" Nothing could equal the astonishment of all
the people at the sight of the strange Woman
riding at the king's right hand. As the rumor
spread amongst the crowd that he had brought
her from the Fatal Mountain, the old and the
prudent shook their heads ominously, and held
their right hands behind them, with the fore and
the little fingers extended ; but all the young and
middle-aged were loud in their praises of her
beauty, and of the grace wherewith she man-
aged her milk-white steed.

" As side by side with Sardanapalus she passed
through the great gate and entered the outer
court, a sharp, rending sound was heard ; and
the pointed summit of the great obelisk which
Ashur had raised long centuries before, crashed
down, splintering the jasper pavement, and sinking deep into the ground.

" But the king did not turn his head. He
heard nothing save the Woman's soft voice.

" When she had dismounted, he led her into
a magnificent hall, and prayed her to repose herself a while. Then, leaving her, he bathed himself in warmed and scented waters ; he caused
his beard and hair to be curled in long ringlets,
according to the custom of his ancestors, which
he had never followed before ; and he arrayed
himself in his most precious robes. And all his

officers and courtiers wondered; for Sardanapalus had hitherto bathed only in water cooled with ice from the frozen mountain peaks, and had paid no heed to the adorning of his person.

"When the king was thus attired, he returned to the hall where he had left the Woman; and presently a sumptuous banquet was served to them, and all the great lords of the kingdom presented the different viands. The old governor was also there; but his eye was dark, and his cheek was pale. It was he who poured out wine to the stranger. As he offered to her the golden goblet, his hand trembled. She drank, and gave it back to him, smiling in his eyes.

"'Serve me ever such wine as that, for I will drink none other,' she said.

"And his heart quailed, for he read in her smile that she had drunk the poison knowingly.

"The deadly draught seemed but to enhance the brilliancy of her beauty. Her eyes flashed brighter under the countless lamps; her lips took a ruddier hue; a lambent flame seemed playing beneath the soft tints of her skin. The king sat like one in a dream, gazing upon her; and all around gazed likewise, spell-bound by her loveliness, — all save the old governor, who had shrunk away in dread.

"But, as the dark hours wore on, the smile

faded upon the Woman's lips. She sighed, and looked wistfully around.

"Sardanapalus entreated to know her wish; and she said to him, —

"'O king! know that I am bound by an oath to spin a certain number of skeins every night. Should the morning dawn ere I had fulfilled my appointed task, my beauty would wither away and my frame shrivel and be consumed like a green bough cast into a fiery furnace.'

"At this, Sardanapalus sprang hastily from the couch whereon he had been reclining, and ordered the wheel of the Fate Amryta to be forthwith brought from the treasury. The wheel was of carven crystal, and there was a tradition that whatever was spun upon it would turn into threads of gold; but so stubborn was it that none within the memory of man had been able to turn it.

"The wheel was brought. When the Woman saw it, she smiled, and ran her fingers over it.

"'It is as I left it,' she said below her breath. But the sound was lost in the humming of the wheel; for, to the wonder of all around, she turned it with the slightest motion of her hand, and the silk they brought her she span into threads of gold.

"As she span, she began to sing again the low

rhyme that the king had heard in the mountain cave; and again, as then, slumber overcame him, and he sank back on the cushions and fell asleep. And she span and sang until the morrow's sun was risen, and all the earth awoke.

"Day by day and night by night passed on, and closer and closer drew the spell about the doomed king. He entered no more the council-chamber, where his great officers attended in vain. Embassies from distant princes were kept ignominiously waiting, and then dismissed without an audience. He bowed no more before the altars of the gods; the priests were forbidden to enter his presence. He studied no longer the welfare of his people, but galled them with taxes, and oppressed them with burdens, that he might squander the revenues of a province upon a single feast. For now there was nought but endless revelling within the palace, the king striving by every display of magnificence to delight the Woman.

"Lapped in luxury, sunk in sloth he lay, while his people murmured and complained, — at first faintly, then louder and louder: but the sound of their discontent, ominous like the distant roar of a rising flood, reached not the ear of the king. He listened but to the one whispering voice.

"So, led by the old governor, with Belesis

and Arsaces, the great lords of the kingdom took counsel together.

"It was night. The city below was hushed in sleep. The cool breeze stole whispering through the trees and flowers of the hanging gardens without, and brought their sweet odors to the chamber where Sardanapalus lay sleeping. The light of the solitary lamp was faintly reflected by the gilded ceiling, and glanced here and there on the projections of the shadowy walls. Beside the lamp sat the Woman in her scarlet robe, spinning bright threads of gold, and singing the unknown rhyme. From time to time she raised her head, as if to listen to some distant sound. At last she smiled, and bent her face over the glittering line that ran fast between her fingers. As she smiled, an invisible door in the wall behind her opened, and shrouded forms crept stealthily forward. As they neared her, with a bound they sprang noiselessly upon her. The great lords of the kingdom held her in a stern and vengeful grip.

"'Hence to hell, Accursed One!' said the old governor; and he aimed the stroke of his dagger at her breast.

"Slowly, and as if repelled by an invisible force, the weapon retreated from the wound, and fell upon the floor at their feet. No blood stained its shining blade; no gash marred the smoothness of the soft, white bosom on which, with staring eyes and blanched faces, the great lords stood gazing. The Woman laughed low. At the sound, they shrank close to each other.

" ' It were easy to send you whence ye should never return,' she said; ' but I will rather that ye tarry yet a while on earth to behold the fulfilment. Now, begone! ' ·

" And, like dogs cowering under the lash " —

Here the Witch suddenly stopped. She rose, and turned her head aside in the attitude of one listening. I also hearkened; but I could hear nothing. As she stood thus, her eyes gave forth flashes of gleaming light, as they had done when she had first perceived me on the plateau at midnight, and her lips parted eagerly.

" Wait for me awhile; I will not tarry," she said.

And, as she spoke the words, she vanished from my sight. The garden seemed to darken as I gazed around.

I sat I know not how long, bewildered and overcome with sudden grief, when a cloud of the strange birds flew fluttering towards me, and, settling on the low branches, began to sing with wonderful trills and cadences, all in harmony one with the other. But, marvellous as was the song, it had no power to cheer me; its sound was hard and false. I knew that no sunlight gladdened the songsters, that no warm nests received them, that no loving mates awaited them, no downy fledglings claimed their care; and I turned impatiently from their sweet, unmeaning warbling.

I looked upward through the branches of the trees. The formless void above filled me with drear disquietude. I longed to see once more the glad light of the sun, the soft glory of the moon and stars.

I glanced at the flowers. Rigid and bold they stared at me. No little thrifty bees or low humming insects fed from their empty cups; no sweet perfume rose incense-like from their blossoms. I remembered the violets and lily-bells of earth, and sighed to behold them again.

I grew restless. The moments seemed to fall like lead upon me. The Witch did not return. Fear lest she had deserted me seized upon me. I felt it impossible to live without the sight of her beauty before my eyes, the sound of her soft whispering voice in my ears. The gardens became hateful to me. I determined to seek for the gate of the treasury, in order to find there some amulet whose virtue might enable me to follow her.

At length I discovered the golden door whereby she had led me into the gardens, and I again entered the treasury. The colossal forms of iron stood as before upon their pedestals, and the walls and vault of polished steel reflected the myriad fires of their eyes.

As I passed along, searching for the charm I coveted, the small black vial, with its violet cloud curling upward, again met my sight. My curiosity returned upon me tenfold. I took it in my hand, and bent my face over it. As I inhaled the vapor, I started and recoiled. So pungent was the odor that my sense could scarcely endure it. But I took courage, and drew it strongly in. The violet cloud spread around me higher and higher, broader and broader: gradually it faded into a pale-gray tint, and then into milky white. It opened; and, looking as into a magic mirror, I beheld my past unrolled before me. I saw my father's castle, the daisy-sprinkled fields whereon I had sported when a child. My little playmates, some dead, some changed, and some forgotten, passed in review before me with the cheery laugh and open brow of other days. I saw my father in his shining mail again, on his roan war-horse, cross the drawbridge the last time he sallied forth; and again my mother sat in her chamber and wept, waiting for the tidings

that never came. Again I saw myself the
orphan heir, surrounded by flatterers and min-
ions, thinking only of what pleasure the day
might bring, caring nothing for the morrow.
The face of an old beggar whom I had repulsed
looked out at me with sorrowful eyes. Again
he stretched forth his withered hand to me; but
I could not give to him, — the time had passed.

Then I beheld myself wearied of my luxurious and thoughtless life, setting forth, a knight-
errant, upon my quest. I saw myself climb the
mountains, mindless of my duty, thinking only
of the Witch. Once more I lay on the plateau
at midnight, and once more the Witch appeared;
but I groaned with horror as I looked upon her.
It was a skeleton form that moved softly towards
my image in the mirror; it was a fleshless hand
that conducted me down the flowery descent
into the magic cave. Shuddering with dread
unspeakable, I saw and knew that it was loathsome, pitiless Death that I had followed.

Still I gazed, and I saw all that had befallen
me in the kingdom of the Demons, until the
mirror showed me myself as I then stood. For
an instant darkness covered my sight; then I
saw myself raise the vial to my lips and drink;
and as my image had done, so also I raised the
vial and drank; and I knew no more until I

found myself lying at the foot of a stone crucifix. Around me were stern and lofty mountains; the sun, red and fiery, was sinking into
the far distance of the western main.

As the remembrance of all that had passed
since I last saw the light of day rushed over
me, I covered my eyes with my hands, and
groaned aloud. Shame, remorse, and horror
mingled their bitterness in one seething cup, and
held it to my shrinking lips. How had I fallen!
What had I become!

Since then five years have passed in bitter
penances and ceaseless prayer. I feel my span
of life fast shrinking. Soon shall I cast off
the heavy burden of my dreadful past. For,
remembering the miracle that brought me up
from the fearful realm wherein, first of all
mortals, my foot has trod, I, even I, most
wretched and guilty of sinners, dare to pray
to the spotless Mother of God to receive, in
that last hour which soon must come, my most
miserable soul.

DOMITIA.

DOMITIA.

WAS born in a far-distant land, beside the Tiber, upon one of the seven hills of Rome. My father was the head of the great house of the Savelli; my mother was Geltrude of Milan. I was their eldest child. Five years after I was born, a little sister came into the world; and after six more of waiting and of prayers, an heir was born, to my parents' great relief, and to the joy of the whole house, and, indeed, I may say of all Rome; for it would have been felt as a misfortune to the city had so ancient a house become extinct.

The Pope sent his chamberlain to congratulate my father, and to bear a precious jewel with his benediction to my mother ; and my father feasted the poor of the city for six successive days.

From that time, the happiness of the palazzo was without a cloud. I look back upon the ensuing years as does a prisoner upon the remembrance of green hills, and smiling gardens, and blue, open skies.

I was always a grave and thoughtful child, and my spirits had hitherto been secretly depressed by the reflection that it was my duty to have been a boy ; but now I became reconciled to my sex, and when I sat beside my mother, and watched her as she played with my little laughing brother, I felt as much happiness as a child's heart can contain.

My sister was very unlike myself. She was a fair and frolicsome child, the favorite of all who saw us, as indeed it was but right that she should be, for she was far more gay and mirthful than I had ever been. But our mother never showed any partiality between us. She seemed to love me as well as she did my sister ; and, even when the heir was born, it diminished in nothing her tenderness and care.

We saw but little of our father. He was always busied in weighty matters, or engaged in the civil feuds which desolated the city. He was a man of proud and distant bearing, and we feared more than we loved him. Our affection was lavished on our mother. As I look back upon her, I thank God for the inestimable blessing of having been tended and nurtured by one so like to an angel.

We lived in Rome during the winter, but, during the summer, at our castle above the Alban Lake. It was always a season of rejoicing to my sister and myself when we saw the long line of covered carts which bore our household gear, escorted by their mounted guard, issue from the massive gate of our palace in Rome, and wind its way across the Campagna, towards our summer stronghold; for, when we were at Rome, our parents lived in great state and ceremony. There were constant entertainments to be given or to be attended, and we saw our mother but at rare intervals. We were left much to the care of our nurse Flavia. She had been my father's foster-mother, and held dearer than aught else the renown and glory of our house. She used, in the long winter evenings, while we sat round the lamp, to tell us stories of the ancient deeds of our forefathers, and of the beauty and grace of our ancestresses. Sometimes she would mingle with these histories legends wild and fearful of the former masters of the city, until we scarcely dared to draw our

breath, and would be undressed and laid in our
beds, silent and shivering with dread. Those
were happy evenings, when our mother would
send for us to come to her tiring-room, and
would talk to us while her women braided her
long hair, and adorned it with jewels and strings
of pearls, and while they attired her in her magnificent robes; but she had little time for us,
and often she would whisper, as she kissed me
good-night, —

"Courage, Leonora mia! the summer will
soon come."

And she was as happy as were my sister and
myself, when she could leave all the pomp of
the city, and retire with us to the hills of Gan-
dolfo, where we were together all the day long,
and no vexatious festival called her from us at
night.

She would sit at her embroidery-frame in the
great window that overlooked the Campagna;
and Cecilia and I would sit on our little
cushions at her feet, and she would teach us
many things, all made sweet to us by her gentle
smile and loving voice. Then, when the heat
of the day was past, she would wander along
the slopes of the hills around, leading us by the
hand, or sit on some mossy stone while we wove
coronals of flowers to deck her fair white brow.

I have never seen any one so beautiful as was my mother.

Around the outer wall of the castle, between the terrace and the moat, were small grated windows which communicated with the dungeons below. It was one of the great pleasures of my sister and myself, to save the daintiest portion of our daily fare, then to creep with it to the terrace, and throw it stealthily down to the prisoners, running away as fast as we could for fear that the guards would see us.

We fancied that they never guessed our errand; but doubtless they had orders from our mother not to interfere with us.

One day we had saved some apricots, and had stolen softly with them to the grating of the dungeon of an old man, who was our especial favorite. As we peeped down, he saw us; and, joining his hands, in the dim twilight below, he implored us by all that we loved best to hasten away, and tell our father that he had found that which was worth his ransom a thousand times over.

We dared not attempt to approach our father, who then chanced to be on one of his rare visits to the castle; but we ran to our mother, and told her all. She went immediately to our father, and, as we learned afterwards from our nurse Flavia, requested leave to send her leech to the old prisoner. Our father, supposing him stricken with illness, consented; and she forthwith despatched the leech — a wise and prudent man, in whom she had great confidence — to the prisoner.

As he followed the keeper of the dungeons down the damp and narrow stone steps, they heard fearful shrieks issuing from the old man's cell. They made all the haste they could; but, ere the keeper could undo the heavy fastenings of the door, the sounds had ceased. When they entered, the old prisoner was lying on his back; his glazing eyes were staring wide in horror; his features were frightfully distorted. They sought to raise him. He was dead.

The dungeon was thoroughly searched, but nothing was found there. This event greatly distressed and terrified my sister and myself, and it was long before we had the courage to pass that side of the terrace; and when the night was closing in, and the wind waved the trees in the castle-garden, we often used to fancy that we heard the death moans of the old prisoner, and would whisper ghastly guesses to each other of the cause of his mysterious end.

But years passed on; and little by little we forgot, as children do, to speak or to think of the old prisoner; little dreaming how fearfully he was to be recalled to our memories, and with what shudderings of terror and anguish we were to receive the key to that buried mystery.

But I must not tarry. It was the summer time. Early one morning my mother and myself, mounted on our Spanish jennets, and attended by our escort, left the castle for a canter around the lake, and through the cool and leafy galleries which lead over the hills towards the villages beyond. We were talking and laughing gayly, as we circled the hollow cup in whose depths lie the placid waters of the lake, when suddenly, from amidst the ruins of the Emperor's villa, which my great grandfather had destroyed in order to build the fortress, rose a kestrel. It soared high into the air above our heads; then, dropping like a stone, it alighted on the head of my mother's horse, and pecked furiously at its eyes.

The blinded animal, maddened by pain and fright, plunged wildly to and fro, unwitting whither it went; then, just as my mother was freeing her foot from the stirrup, in order to leap from its back, it sprang towards the precipitous bank, tottered, and rolled down the steep declivity, bearing her with it.

I cannot dwell on this great anguish. Few words must suffice me now.

She was borne to the castle, and laid upon her bed. She still breathed faintly; but we knew that her hour had come. Mercifully, her consciousness did not return. She was spared the last farewell.

We knelt, weeping and praying, about the bed, until the leech, who had his hand upon her pulse, laid it down reverently by her side. Then our sobs and tears broke forth unrestrained; and the priest advanced to bless her lifeless clay. But, as he stood before her, her eyelids were suddenly lifted, revealing a look so fierce, so haughty, that he started back in terror. We sprang to our feet, and crowded around her. With an impatient motion of her hand she waved us away, and, slowly rising, stood upon her feet.

She cast her eyes gloomily around her, then walked to her inner room, entered, and closed the door.

My sister and myself stood gazing in consternation upon each other. Could this indeed be our gentle, gracious mother? Had she been snatched from the jaws of death to be given back to us thus changed?

The priest was the first to speak. He ap-

proached us, and, in an uncertain and troubled
tone, begged us to come, with all the household,
to the chapel, there to give thanks for our
mother's preservation. White and anxious, we
obeyed.

The chapel was but dimly lighted by its narrow windows, cut high in the walls. Before
the altar burned four great waxen tapers. The
air was so damp — for the chapel was partly
under-ground — that each candle seemed surrounded by a small, yellow cloud.

The priest began to recite the consecrated
words of thanksgiving, but his face was pale,
and his voice trembled as it left his lips; and
the responses of the assembled household, kneeling before him, rose on the chilly air like
groans.

When the service of thanksgiving was over,
I took my sister's hand, and went with her to
the door of our mother's apartments. We
knocked softly. She did not answer. We tried
the lock; it was fastened from within. We
listened. We heard a faint, tapping sound. It
ceased, then re-commenced. It seemed to come
from different parts of the chamber in turn.
There was something in the sound that frightened us still more. The servants gradually
assembled at a little distance from us. They,

too, heard the low sound. They whispered to each other below their breath.

At last the hour of the mid-day meal sounded ; and the *maestro di casa*, with his wand, came to announce to my mother, as was his office, that she was served.

As he ended, the sound ceased ; then, after a little pause, the door was thrown open, and our mother appeared on the threshold. She seemed to tower above our heads, so haughty was her bearing. Her eyes, once so soft, had now a cold and cruel stare ; her lips, whose wont it was to be so smiling, were now compressed and stern. She moved on with a stately step, passing my sister and myself without a glance. We followed her, as she swept slowly down the corridor, and timidly took our accustomed places beside her at the table. She frowned.

" Draw back, ye little apes," she said. And, the tears streaming down our cheeks, we rose, and took our seats at the foot of the table.

Our mother looked with a mixture of curiosity and disgust upon the viands on the table. There was only one dish that she tasted. It was composed of lampreys stewed with honey and spices ; and the manner of its preparation was a secret handed down among the servants of the *credenza.*

She demanded Falernian wine to drink; nor did she once touch to her lips the water which formed her habitual beverage.

When the meal was ended,— Cecilia and myself had eaten nothing,— our mother rose, and returned to her own apartments.

My sister and myself had no longer courage to follow her. We went to the room which we shared together, and there abandoned ourselves to all the agony of our grief.

When we grew calmer, and I was able to reflect, I came to the conclusion that this sudden and unaccountable change in our mother must be the result of the shock she had received; and, after bathing my eyes, and composing my demeanor, I ordered the leech to be summoned.

He had lived in the castle ever since I was a child; and I had a great affection for him. But, when he appeared, with his kind and compassionate look, I knew not how to frame the questions I wished to ask. My sister sat weeping by my side, and her affliction gradually melted away all my self-command; and I began to weep also, not having been able to say a word.

"My gracious young lady," he said at length, seeing me incapable of explaining why I had summoned him, and knowing but too well the cause, "let not your mind be disturbed by the contemplation of a phenomenon which, in its nature, is but temporary. The vital spirits of the Princess have received so great a shock as to be for the moment displaced; and those which belong to the spleen and the liver have gone to the brain. But this disturbance is accidental; and the balance will soon be restored by the healing power of Nature. Meantime, I earnestly pray you, that your affection for the Princess, your mother, may not incline you to lay too much stress upon any casual differences in her deportment; for it is not to her daughter that I need say, that God never before assembled such a multitude of excellent and lovely graces in a human form as he has deigned to show to the world in the person of that most exalted lady, your mother."

Having said this, and perceiving me to be somewhat comforted by his words, the leech withdrew.

But, alas! neither the morrow nor the next day, nor all the days that followed, saw the hoped-for change in our mother. We seemed to be living in a dream; our former life had disappeared, and, with it, all our pleasures and happiness were gone. No more did we sit at her feet, and learn wisdom from her gentle lips; no more did we wander by her side over the green hills, no more weave gay flowers into garlands to deck her head. We were forbidden to approach her presence; and, did she ever chance to meet us wandering disconsolately through the silent corridors, she would scowl at us, and bid us to our chamber. On our little brother only did she ever smile; but, strange to say, the child, who had hitherto adored her, now shrieked whenever he was brought before her, giving every sign of the utmost terror and dislike.

She never confessed nor went to mass. She was imperious and exacting towards everybody; so difficult to please, that her women trembled whenever their duties summoned them to attend her. But the greater part of the time she spent shut up alone in her apartments; and then again was constantly heard the same low tapping.

So weeks passed on, each day seeming more dreadful than the last. My little sister pined and faded; her gayety was all gone. She would sit silent, hour after hour, looking on the ground, the tears stealing down her cheeks, until I would take her in my arms, and we would weep together.

Our father was away, warring with the Pope

against Venice; the old priest had no comfort
to give us; the leech, when we questioned him,
only shook his head, and bade us pray and try
to hope. We prayed, earnestly and constantly;
but we had lost the power to hope.

I have said that my mother never confessed
nor heard the mass; but something even more
dreadful I discovered at this time.

In one of the great halls of the castle, among
the ancient statues ranged along the walls, was
a small bronze figure of Mercury, greatly prized
by our father because of its delicate workmanship, and the precious jewels which formed its
eyes. One day this disappeared, nor could any
one tell what had become of it. It was in its
accustomed place at night, and in the morning
it was gone. There was great grief and distress
through the castle at its loss; for all the servants
and retainers feared that they might be suspected
of having stolen it.

Among the changed habits of our mother was
this, — she would allow no one to enter her oratory. She would often shut herself up there,
and sing strange songs that we had never heard
before. The priest was one day passing, and he
stayed to listen; but all at once he crossed himself, stopped his ears, and hastened away. He
forbade any one in the castle, for the future, to

pass through that gallery; nor would he ever tell what it was that he had heard.

One day Flavia came to me with her finger upon her lips, and whispered to me to follow her. She led me to a room in which the linen was kept. It was built in a projecting angle of the court-yard, and on one side was a high, lozenge-shaped window. She badé me mount upon a table under this window, and look out. I did as she told me, and saw that the window commanded across the court-yard a view of the interior of my mother's oratory. But all within was changed. The great ebony crucifix lay on the ground; the picture of St. Catherine of Sienna, on which I had gazed with reverence ever since my infancy, had been torn down; the bowl of holy water had disappeared; and the books of devotion were cast in a heap on one side. In the centre of the room, upon an antique altar of carved ivory, which had formerly served my mother as a stand for flowers, stood the little bronze statue of Mercury; and before it was a basket containing a piece of honeycomb, and a vase filled with what looked like milk. My mother sat in front of the statue. I saw her lips moving, but I could hear nothing; the distance was too great.

As I gazed upon this unexpected sight, the

room grew indistinct, and every thing seemed wavering about me. Then I felt old Flavia's arms clasp me; and the next thing I knew I was lying on the floor, and she was rubbing my hands.

When I recovered, I remained for a while as if stunned. I could scarcely bring myself to believe that the pious hands, which had so often clasped my own, and held them up in supplication to the holy Virgin and the blessed Jesus, had prepared that pagan offering, and performed those sacrilegious rites; that those pure lips, whose daily wont it had been to chant sweet hymns of gratitude and praise, could be perverted to the deadly sin of breathing forth adoration to a heathen god of bronze. The horrible thought that my mother had forfeited her salvation, that her soul was for ever lost, filled me with unutterable grief and terror.

When I could speak, I bade Flavia, who was rapidly telling her beads, say what cause she could imagine for all that was so dreadful and so strange. And she, looking fearfully around, said that not only she herself, but all the household, were persuaded that her mistress had been bewitched by the kestrel; and that old Rinaldino was watching night and day, hidden among the bushes by the lake, hoping to bring it down with his cross-bow. For, that if it were killed and cooked, and my mother should eat but the tiniest morsel of its flesh, the enchantment would be broken, and she would become as she was before.

But, although Flavia's faith in the bewitchment was firm, I was not persuaded; nor did old Rinaldino ever bring home the kestrel, so that the experiment could never be tried.

I made Flavia promise that she would tell no one of the unholy rites in my mother's oratory; and she kept her word. It remained a secret, known but to us two alone.

The strange tappings, which so constantly sounded from my mother's apartments, at length ceased, to our great relief; for, incessant though they had been, none of the household could ever become accustomed to the sounds, and they continually alarmed every one. But, after a few days of quiet, our mother ordered another suite of rooms on the same side of the house to be prepared for her, and she took possession of them when they were ready. No sooner was she established in her new apartments, than the strange, tapping sound began again, greatly disturbing all in the castle. Once the priest came in his consecrated robes, and brought holy water, and sprinkled it on the door, and said the awful form of exorcism; but the faint, unremitting tappings went on all the while, and continued after he had ceased; and he went away shaking his head.

So time went on. One night I could not sleep. My sister and myself had always of late retired at sundown. It was less painful to be in our own room together, than to be wandering in the great unlighted halls below, or standing at the door of our mother's apartment, never opened to us now. Cecilia was quietly sleeping by my side; but I was lying plunged in mournful thought, when I heard some one enter the room beside us, — old Flavia's. The door leading into our chamber was ajar, and I heard all that passed.

"What! are you already a-bed, Flavia mia?" said the voice of Caterina, one of my mother's tiring-women. "Much peace may you find there! Know ye not that now-a-days the whole household is afraid to sleep? Half of us watch, while the other half take their rest. Who knows what may happen, any night, ere morning? And the days are bad enough, the saints know. What think you! yesterday, as I was braiding the Princess's hair, I did not arrange it to suit her, and she caught up the long golden bodkin which lay on the table before her, and plunged

it a full inch into my breast, and she menaced
Camilla with being thrown into the lake to feed
the fishes because she fastened on a bow awry."

"Heaven defend us!" exclaimed Flavia.
"Surely we have need to pray that old Rinaldino
may speedily bring down the kestrel, to end this
accursed spell."

"Of course we do," replied Caterina. "We
pray morning, noon, and night. It is no time to
neglect the saints when people are in danger of
their lives."

"But tell me, what was it about the merchant
yesterday?" inquired Flavia. "I was here with
my gracious young ladies, and saw and heard
nothing."

"It was strange enough!" answered the
tiring-woman. "The Princess saw him from
her window, as he entered the court-yard, and
ordered that he should bring his goods to her.
She tossed them over scornfully, though he had
the most exquisite head-tires, and silks, and vel-
vets for bodices, and laces and embroideries,
that were ever seen; nor would she allow the
poor man to say a word in praise of his wares.
At his first sentence, she fastened such a look
upon him that he stammered and drew back,
and stood mute, until she asked him what it was
that he had in a drawer that he had not opened.

He said that it was something he had bought from a peasant, — an antique lyre. She commanded him to show it instantly; and he produced a discolored piece of ivory, curiously carved with eagles' heads and foliage work, with all the strings gone. The Princess immediately bought it, and ordered him to carry away all the rest of his merchandise; and she forthwith despatched a messenger to Rome, for a goldsmith, and commanded that he should bring gold wire; and he has been at work all to-day."

As she spoke, a strain of music floated up through the open window, so strange in its intonations that I had never listened to the like; and I heard from below my mother's voice, singing in cadence; but I could not catch the words. It was a low, irregular chant, at times swelling into a fierce, vindictive wail. My flesh crept as I lay hearkening to it.

"Holy Virgin! whoever heard such sounds as those?" exclaimed Caterina, in affright. "How shall I ever dare to go through the corridors to my own room! Thank Heaven that it is not my night to disrobe the Princess. I would rather walk barefoot over red-hot ploughshares. But I must go. The longer I tarry the more afraid I shall be."

And I heard her timid foot-fall die along the echoing length of the gallery.

The strange measure ceased after a while, but still I could not sleep. Midnight tolled from the great watch-tower, and still I had not closed my eyes, when I fancied I heard a muffled tread passing along the corrider. I sat up in bed, and distinctly saw a gleam of light shoot along the ground, shining from beneath my door. I rose hurriedly, threw a robe over my shoulders, and, when I could no longer hear the footsteps nor see the light, I noiselessly unclosed the door and passed out into the gallery.

I followed softly the direction the footsteps had taken ; at length I saw a faint beam before me. Still more cautiously I pursued my way. I tracked it to the chapel. I paused and looked in as I gained the door. The chapel was empty. The moonbeams streamed down from the narrow and lofty windows, and showed a black opening before the altar, where a stone had been raised and laid aside. I advanced and looked down. At my feet, I saw a rapidly descending passage. The faint light of the moonbeams showed but its opening, then it lost itself in utter darkness.

I drew back an instant, then, with a prayer to the blessed Madonna to protect me, I entered the subterranean way. I was obliged to grope my steps, holding by the side wall, for I could see nothing. I walked in this manner a long while, always going deeper and deeper into the earth, as I perceived by the rapidly descending slope. At length I saw from below a faint, grayish light. I pressed on, and finally arrived at the extremity of the passage.

Hidden myself, I looked without. Before me lay the calm, still waters of the lake. Between rose the crumbling foundations of Domitian's villa, with scattered blocks of stone heaped upon one another, half-covered by rank weeds and clambering vines. But my eye rested only an instant on these. There was that before my sight which riveted it.

Upon a broken column, the moonlight shining full upon her, sat my mother. On the ground before her crouched a withered, witch-like form.

"Speak, counsel me!" said my mother, in the harsh, commanding tones now habitual to her. "Ye were crafty once; at my behest be crafty yet again."

"Yes, once," answered the croaking voice of the hag; "but how can I now propitiate him who inspires with craft? His temples are ruins, his altars are cast down."

"Not all," replied my mother. "Milk and honey still send up their pleasant odors to his nostrils. Mercury, O favorable god, listen and hear ! "

And she clasped her hands, and looked upward to the silent sky.

I pressed tightly on my heart to still its throbbings, and bent my ear again.

" Ye have searched in the private chambers so far with no reward," said the old woman ; "yet ye are certain that it lies towards the north ? "

" Most certain," replied my mother. " He would not dare deceive me."

" And ye have by night sounded the walls and floor of the halls below, and still have found nothing ? "

" Ye know it," answered my mother, in her imperious voice.

The hag sunk her head upon her knees, and pondered awhile in silence. Then she rose, gathered up some pebbles, which she carefully examined, rejecting many, and replacing them with others. This done, she climbed upon a heap of stones that rose out of the lake, and, repeating a low chant, threw them in, one by one. The last fell from her hand. There was silence ; then, mournfully rising from the opposite bank of the lake, came the cry of an owl. The creature hooted three times, then twice, and again once.

The hag chuckled, and, rubbing her hands together, returned to my mother, who still sat on the ruined column.

"Ye heard," she said. "Did you understand?"

"I heard," replied my mother; "but am I a loathsome witch, to understand?"

"Nay, great as ye are, ye have need of old Catta," rejoined the old woman, laughing hideously.

"Cease prating, and expound to me," said my mother, scowling.

"Look in the dungeons, O august one!" answered her companion. "Minerva herself assures you that you shall find it there."

My mother rose.

"I'll reckon with you, sorceress, should you have told me false."

"Nay, mighty one," whined the hag, "have I not many a time merited and received reward from those hands? Have ye forgotten who it was that, when Domitian"—

"Hush!" interrupted my mother, stamping her foot and clenching her hand; "ye make me wish for that same dagger now."

The hag cowered down among the stones, and my mother turned away towards the entrance of the subterranean passage.

As I saw her coming towards me, I felt every limb turn into ice; then the blood made a rush in my veins, and I fled up the passage. I gained the chapel; I flew through the corridors; reached my own room, locked the door, and barred it with the articles of furniture nearest at hand; then sank upon the ground with a hope that I was dreaming. But again the stealthy footsteps and the glimmering lamp glided past, and then I knew that all was true.

I lay, I know not how long, before I rose and crept shivering to my bed. I folded the sleeping child in my arms as if to shield her. She nestled close to me, and kissed me in her slumber. After this I remember nothing save one long, frightful night, during which I seemed to be ever falling from the brink of some precipice, or hunted by beasts of prey, or buried in the subterranean passage, or drowning in the waters of the lake.

At last my consciousness returned: but I found myself too weak to speak or to move. I could see through my half-closed lids that I was in my own room, but that my sister was no longer beside me. Old Flavia sat sleeping in a chair at the foot of the bed; a night-lamp was burning in the corner. Eleven o'clock struck, — midnight, — still Flavia slept on.

As I lay, I heard again the stealthy footsteps, and again I saw the gleam of light pass beneath my door.

I felt a wave of feverish strength run through me. I rose, and, creeping from the room, I followed as before. Again I passed through the dark passages to the chapel; the gaping stone stood open; down the subterranean way I pursued my mother. I looked out again upon the gleaming waters of the waveless lake. I saw her again sitting among the ruins, and before her stood the hag. Through the stillness the sound of their voices came again, clear and distinct to my ear.

"And still it remains hidden?" my mother was saying.

"Sealed in a hollow stone, beneath the highest step leading to the vestibule," repeated the old woman. "It would puzzle the architect himself to say where that is now."

And she glanced around on the ruins with a low laugh.

"Peace with your jests!" said my mother, sternly. "Your business is to listen to one who allows small comment."

The hag shrank back.

"I have searched every cranny of the fortress save one," she continued, "and that I shall

examine to-night. And now follow me. We
will explore it together."

I turned as she rose, and sped up the passage
till I reached the chapel. There I hid myself
behind the altar and waited.

Presently I heard the footsteps of my mother
and the old woman. As they ascended into the
chapel, I heard the hag sniff the air.

" Do I not scent human breath?" she said.

And my mother answered, —

" Not a soul in the castle but sleeps. The sen-
tinels on the outer wall alone wake at this hour."

They left the chapel, and I followed them
through many windings not known to me
before; for I had never been allowed to go
into this part of the castle. At length they
passed through a heavy door, and down a flight
of stone steps. When I had reached the foot of
the steps, looking out from the shadow of an
angle, I saw her apply a master-key to the door
of a cell. They passed within. I stole to the
door and looked.

My mother drew a small bronze dagger from
her girdle, and tapped in succession upon each
stone. Each returned the same dull sound.
Around the walls, over the floor she moved,
tapping gently upon every separate block. The
hag stood watching her.

The lamp upon the floor shed its faint light
upon my mother's stately, white-robed figure,
and dimly showed the wrinkled hideousness of
the old woman.

Suddenly my mother smote upon a stone
beneath the grated window. I heard a sound
different from all that had preceded it, — a faint
tramping, a low wailing, as of a distant multitude hurrying to and fro, in fear and dread,
below the ground.

She flung down the dagger and stood erect,
her eyes blazing like those of a tiger when it
sees its coveted prey. The old woman sprang
forward with the lamp, and bent over the
stone. She scratched away the mould that
covered it.

"Here is the sign in very truth, O august
one!" she said. "Now let us raise it."

And she sought with her bony fingers to draw
it from its cavity. She paused, after striving in
vain, and muttered low curses.

My mother bent over it, and examined it for
a moment.

"See you not the Christian sign, made by the
slaves who placed it here?" she exclaimed.

The hag drew back in terror. "We can
never raise it," she said. "O mighty one!
leave this place. I feel already the torments.

Come, let us go." She caught hold of the folds of my mother's dress.

"Peace, fool!" said my mother, frowning upon her companion. "Shall Domitia tremble because of your grovelling fears? Speak, say what will avail to raise the stone?"

"The hand of a Christian only," stammered the hag, looking fearfully at the block.

"I have not far to seek," said my mother. "That fair-haired child will suit my purpose well."

And she moved towards the door.

I tarried no longer in the shadow without. I advanced, and stood before them.

The old hag turned her bleared and evil eyes upon me. My mother towered up as if about to crush me into the earth.

· "O thou that bearest the semblance of my mother!" I said, "behold I offer to your need the hand of a Christian maiden to raise the stone. That fulfilled, I adjure you, by the living God, vanish, and disquiet my father's house no more."

My mother shivered as I spoke, and the old hag cowered and moaned.

I moved onward to the stone. I signed three times over it the holy cross, then raised it from its bed. When I lifted it, again I heard the faint

trampling, the low wailing, as of a distant multitude, rushing to and fro in fear and dread,
below the ground.

As I gave it into my mother's hands, I saw
that her form had begun to fade and grow indistinct, and that of the old woman also. As I
stood, they became fainter and fainter. At
length I could see the lines of the stone wall
through .their transparent figures. So, slowly
and without a word they vanished, bearing with
them the close-sealed stone with its hidden
secret.

When their last trace had vanished, I knelt on
the dungeon floor and prayed. And as I prayed
I heard, as it were within my soul, a voice, saying, —

" My child, you have given me rest. My
mortal body now will be undisturbed. The
gates of paradise are opening to my soul."

I felt an air-pressed kiss upon my forehead.
Then there was silence and stillness all around.

As the stars began to fade, I regained my
chamber. Flavia still slept. I lay down upon
my bed, and waited till the day had fully
dawned ; then I wakened her, and ordered her
to dress me and lead me to my mother's apartments. With many wondering and apprehensive
words she obeyed.

The door was locked. I commanded it to be forced. The whole household was gathered around.

When the door at length yielded, we entered. Within, upon her bed, lay my mother, as we had placed her, when we brought her up, dying, from the borders of the lake. A gentle, radiant smile was on her face, a look as of a reflection from eternal peace.

With stifled cries and ejaculations the more timid shrank back, while the bolder, softly drawing near, stood and gazed and wept.

The priest advanced and blessed the lovely, lifeless clay ; and, as he spoke, the morning sun rose, and its rays streamed through the open window and rested on her face, sweet and gracious as that of one of God's holy angels.

All day, with my little sister and brother, I knelt beside our mother ; and, when the night came, we buried her in the chapel ; and over the tomb our father raised a monument to her who rests in God.

OMBRA.

O M B R A.

HE time had come when it behooved me to leave my home. The pleasant days of childhood lay behind me; I must leave the broad lands and stately castle wherein they had been passed: henceforth my thought must be how to quit me of my *devoir* as a knight, to succor the oppressed, bring comfort to the afflicted, and to die, if need be, in the giant strife of Right against Might. My father gave me, kneeling before him, his blessing; and, though his stately and self-contained demeanor betrayed no emotion, yet I saw his chest heave, and a cloud dim the piercing eyes that still looked forth, falcon keen, from beneath their heavy white eyebrows.

My step-mother, fair and fawning, sitting beside him, smiled, and bade me make sure I should be remembered in her daily prayers to the Virgin. And so I left my home.

After leaving the castle, I rode on for some days without meeting any thing worthy of note. The sky was clear, the way was pleasant, and my hopes were high. But, on the seventh afternoon, the sun, which had risen that morning lowering and angry, hid itself behind heavy and ominous clouds; the wind moaned and sobbed in the distance. I saw the birds precipitately seeking shelter, some of them flying in circles high in the air, as if bewildered, and uttering discordant screams; while others were darting close to the ground, their disturbed and hurried flight proclaiming their fears.

I looked around for refuge, but found none. Not a castle nor tower was in sight. The wind rose higher; its wail was changing into a sullen whisper, prophetic of the coming outburst of its wrath. The clouds had gathered each moment deeper, till now they covered the sky with a uniform sheet of leaden gray, varied here and there with white and ragged ledges, from within which gleamed at intervals a phosphorescent light.

I saw at a distance, on a hill-side, what looked

like a deserted quarry. Thither I decided to betake myself, in the cheerless hope of finding some cranny wherein I might hide me from the approaching storm. But, ere I had accomplished half the distance, the tempest burst upon me in all its fury. The rain descended in torrents, obscuring my sight of all save the objects nearest me; the lightning glared from every quarter of the heavens at once, and the thunder crashed over my head; while the howling and shrieking of the blast completed the horror of the scene.

I battled on against the storm for some time as best I could; but, as I approached the quarry, I became completely bewildered, and was about relinquishing all hope of finding protection, when a sudden flash of lightning revealed at a little distance a ruinous-looking hut, built against the steep side of the hill. I hastened towards it with all the speed of which my terrified horse was capable; and, springing to the ground, I knocked loudly at the door, which, as well as the window, seemed strongly secured. After a short pause the window-shutter was cautiously opened, and an old woman with a most villanous face peered stealthily out at me. She returned no reply to my urgent request for entrance, but studied my appearance carefully, her eye resting for an unreasonable length of

time, as it seemed to me, on the jewelled fastening of my plume. At length she retired from
the window; I heard voices within; then the
door was opened, but not by her. A girl of
about sixteen, of singular beauty, though most
sullen expression, appeared on the threshold,
and bade me enter while she provided for my
steed. I answered her discourteous address
gently, and expressed the desire to myself see
to the accommodation of the horse. She turned
without speaking; and, following her as she led
the way around the foot of a projecting cliff,
I found myself in face of the quarry I had been
seeking.

She pointed out to me a narrow crevice, which,
entering to a considerable depth, would afford
protection to my horse against the descending
flood. As she stood close to the animal's head,
a new flash, of such vividness as to almost blind
me, burst from the sky; and the horse, making
an abrupt movement of affright, struck the steel
barb of his frontlet upon her arm. As I saw
the blood start forth, I tore off my dripping
scarf and bound it around the injured limb.

The girl stood sullenly mute, not answering a
word to my expressions of regret; but, as I released her arm, she raised her eyes and gave
me a sudden look, — a look which I did not then

comprehend, but whose meaning was soon disclosed to me.

She reconducted me to the hut, the old woman carefully rebarring the door behind me. While the girl employed herself in kindling a fire, I looked around me to examine, as well as the dim twilight which made its way through the crevices of the door and window allowed, what place I had chanced upon.

It seemed but a common peasant's hut, the furniture consisting only of a pallet bed, a large wooden table, and some stools: a large pile of straw was heaped in one corner. I saw nothing to disquiet me; and yet I found, after the first feeling of relief at being sheltered from the storm raging without, a vague sense of insecurity stealing over me. I looked at the old woman, who, seated on a low stool, her hands clasped around her knees, had not ceased to contemplate me since I entered; and from her my eyes turned to the lithe and rounded figure of the girl, and I smiled at myself for my causeless and irrational disquietude: nevertheless, reason with it as I would, it incessantly returned upon me, till I flushed with anger at my own folly, yet yielded to the feeling so far as to retain my armor entire.

The girl, meantime, had prepared for me a

most savory meal, such as I had little anticipated from the appearance of the hut. She warmed some rich broth, which she set before me, and produced from a covered shelf the remains of a venison pasty, a half loaf of white bread, and a flask of wine. Then she stood leaning against the wall, her head sunk on her breast, her eyebrows drawn low over her eyes.

I thanked her for her courtesy, and begged of her to seat herself and eat with me. With an abrupt gesture she refused. Nevertheless, she seemed to change her mind; for a few moments later she approached the table as if to alter the disposition of the viands before me; and, standing so as to hide what she did from the old woman, she broke a crumb of bread from the morsel I was eating, and carried it to her mouth. It seemed to me that in a dream I had seen that same motion before.

"Has the young lord good wine? the right wine?" asked the old woman, bending forward and peering at the flask beside me.

"Not yet," replied the girl; "I keep that for the last."

And as she spoke she filled my glass anew with wine; then, producing a second flask, she filled another glass, while the old woman watched her covertly.

"This is a better wine," said the girl, addressing me for the first time since I entered; but, as she spoke, she interposed her figure between the table and the old woman, and adroitly substituted the first glass for the second, which she bore away and deposited upon the shelf.

"A better wine," repeated the old woman, rubbing her hands together with a low, chuckling laugh.

I drained the glass, then, lowering my visor, threw myself down upon the pallet bed which the girl had been shaking up for me.

"Feign sleep, whatever happens," she muttered below her breath as she passed near me, bearing away the fragments left from my supper.

I closed my eyes, and lay in no enviable frame of mind. All the strange and sinister tales that I had heard in my childhood returned upon my mind, blending with the wailing of the wind, and slow, continuous falling of the rain without, — for, although the fury of the storm had passed, the elements had not yet sunk to rest, — and with the light step of the girl within as she moved backwards and forwards.

At length I heard the voice of the old woman.

"Go kindle the fire in yonder," she said. "It is high time, and now there is no danger. It will be long ere he wakes again," and she laughed. "My fingers itch to handle those rubies. What ailed him to go to sleep in his helmet?" she grumbled querulously. "But I shall not need to wait long."

As she ended, I heard a rustling, and, looking from between my lids, I saw the girl remove the pile of straw which lay in the corner; and behind it I beheld a large, low aperture in the wall. She stooped and disappeared through it. After a while I saw light shine forth. A long time elapsed; finally the girl returned. As she reappeared, the old woman addressed her.

"Pepita, I am thirsty. Give me the glass of wine you took from the stranger. It will turn sour if it remain there open."

The girl moved slowly and hesitatingly towards the covered shelf. She took down the glass, but stumbled as she carried it towards the old woman, and the wine was spilt upon the ground.

"A thousand curses on you!" exclaimed the old witch. "Such good wine! such excellent wine! and all gone to waste."

And she berated the girl angrily; but the girl made no reply.

Whilst she was still scolding, I heard the approaching sound of many feet. The girl rapidly untwisted the scarf from her arm and

threw it into a corner; then, again passing near
me, she muttered, —

"Feign sleep."

The door was hastily opened in reply to three
sharp raps; and, looking as before between my
half-closed lids, I saw a band of pilgrims, in
brown robes and broad hats with scallop shells,
enter. There were twelve of them: one had
the swarthy complexion and lustreless black hair
of a Moor.

The party suddenly hushed their voices as
they came in, and one of them whispered, —

"What's this, flesh or fowl?"

"You need not whisper," said the old woman.
"He has had the stirrup cup. He has started
on a long journey. He will meet a numerous
company. Ha, ha!"

"Perhaps, if he hurries," rejoined one of the
pilgrims, "he may catch up with the Caballero
we despatched to find his forefathers this afternoon. But stay, he seems a dainty youth, judg-
ing from his array, — he will scarce relish the
travel in company with that vinegar-faced gentle-
woman who gave her last scream at the same
time."

And the pilgrims laughed in hideous chorus.
Then they approached and stood around me as
I lay shrouded in my armor.

"Stay, Bernardino," said one of the burliest of the band, "that armor will serve your turn well. Yours is not so well jointed as it might be. I thought you were done for last week, when that squire's blade so nearly pinked you under the corselet."

"Yes," answered a younger voice, "I shall fit into it like the meat of an egg into its shell. Let's have it off now, and throw him down at once."

At this an almost irrepressible impulse rushed over me to spring to my feet and sell my life as dearly as possible; but, as he ended, the girl came forward, and lifted her sullen eyes to his.

"I won't have any more thrown down until they don't know what's done with them. I had bad dreams for a week after the last one. I kept hearing his shriek when he sank under the water. Wait till after supper: that will be time enough."

The younger pilgrim seemed inclined to dispute; but the rest interfered, and, saying it was of no consequence whether it were done an hour sooner or later, demanded clamorously their supper forthwith; and one by one they passed through the aperture, followed by the old woman, and left me alone.

When thus freed from observation, I turned on

my side, and, approaching my eyes to the loosely constructed wall of stone, looked through a crevice that was near me.

I saw a spacious cavern dimly lighted by the blaze of an enormous fire, the smoke of which rose in circling clouds and hung in a thick mass above. Near the fire was a long oaken table, and round it sat the pilgrims. They had thrown aside their robes and hats, and I saw that they were all cased in steel and armed to the teeth. The table was covered with silver, and to my horror I recognized the hallowed dishes and chalices wherein the Holy Sacrament is administered to man.

The girl and the old woman rapidly set before the band the smoking viands, and served them with wine; while the robbers jeered and jested at them, and in coarse and brutal wise bade them hurry.

Then the revel began. Loud and long were their songs; furious was their mirth; too horrible to remember, the deeds they recounted and gloried in. Occasionally a quarrel would burst out between some two or three of them; but to this the others paid no heed, taking it, as it would .seem, as a matter of course. Looking again through the crevice, I saw the girl pour out wine to the Moor. He caught her by the wrist.

"Nay, Judas!" shouted the rest of the band, "no scruples. Don't bring your old tricks here. Down with the forbidden drink!"

And with hoots and yells they all rose and precipitated themselves upon the Moor, to force him to drink the wine.

Profiting by the universal clamor and confusion, the girl glided rapidly into the outer hut where I lay. She returned without a word; and I saw, as I peered through the crevice, that she bore back a flask of wine, which she placed in a corner without any one's seeming to notice her.

At last, their object effected, the tumult was appeased, and the robbers resumed their seats around the table. The girl threw on the fire a fresh armful of brushwood, which, instantly kindling, flamed upward, sending out a shower of sparks. Its light was reflected by the gleaming armor and burnished silver, and played on the desperate and savage faces of the company, distorted by their brawl and reddened by their copious draughts of wine.

"Come, Pepita," said the oldest of the band, "fill us once more our cups. The master will soon be here, and we must finish betimes."

At this the girl drew forth the flask from the corner and rapidly filled the chalice beside each robber; then, holding high the consecrated vases, they shouted forth a ribald and impious song. At its close each drained his cup.

But no sooner had they swallowed the wine than they began to mutter incoherently; their heads fell from side to side; they seemed over-whelmed by sudden stupor. Some of them slipped down from their seats and lay along the ground; others sank heavily forward on the dishes that covered the table. The girl stood steadily watching them. I saw by the light of the blaze that her face had turned quite white.

The old woman meantime had stolen into a corner, and was there draining what remained in the flask. But, as she still held it to her lips, I saw her head fall, and she sank back.

In the sudden silence which had succeeded to the wild uproar within, I beheld the girl bend forward and raise her hand to her ear as if to catch a distant sound. I, too, listened, and heard the faint echo of a horse's hoofs. She caught up a small lamp. In an instant she was at my side.

"Up, up!" she said. "Now it all rests with you."

I started to my feet and grasped my sword. The girl unbarred the door.

The sounds came rapidly nearer. I heard the

rattling of armor without; a rider springing from his horse; the door was thrown open, and a form of gigantic height entered, clothed in complete panoply of steel.

"Hell-cat!" he shouted, as he crossed the threshold, turning to the girl; and, quick as lightning, he hurled his dagger at her; then, without a moment's pause, he rushed upon me.

The fight was an unequal one. Though perhaps his match in skill, his great height gave him the superiority over me. He constantly overreached my guard; and had not my armor been of proved Milan steel, his sword would have pierced it more than once. At length, pressing me harder and harder, he bore me to my knee, and, shortening his sword, was about to deal what would have been a fatal blow, when, glancing upward, I saw a descending gleam of light; and, with a dying yell, my enemy fell, face forward, a dagger plunged deep in his neck.

The girl stood over him, her hair streaming back, her eyes blazing.

She spurned him with her foot.

"At length, hound!—at length!" she said.

She turned to me.

"Hence!"

And she moved towards the door. I followed her, panting, dizzy, mechanically muttering thanks to God.

The storm had ceased, the rising moon lay peacefully over the landscape without. As I stood, the night wind bore to my ear, faint, yet distinct, the sound of a distant bell.

"Yes, there," said the girl. "But wait, old Juanita, — she must not stay."

And she went back into the hut. I accompanied her, as, bearing the little lamp, she passed the bleeding corpse and returned into the cavern.

The fire had almost gone out. A few brands yet glowed amid the ashes, faintly revealing dark, heavy forms stretched motionless around the table.

"Juanita!" she called, but there was no reply.

"The old woman drank also," I said, and pointed to the corner where the prostrate figure was lying. She stood and gazed upon it.

"She beat me when I was a child," she said; "but that was long ago."

Then, addressing me, —

"What is done when Christians die?" she asked.

I told her how their bodies were composed for their last sleep, with closed lids and folded hands, and burning tapers at their feet: and she

knelt beside the old woman and arranged her as
I had said ; then, placing the little lamp at her
feet, she turned away.

"Yes, there," she repeated. "How often
have I listened to those bells!"

She took a brand from the fire to give her
light, and went to another side of the cave.
Presently she came back, bearing a golden pix.

"It is my entrance gift," she said. "Now
hence!"

And we passed out from the cavern with its
dead, and forth again into the cool, free air.

Led by her, I proceeded down a rugged way
until I arrived at the border of a vast lake. On
its opposite side rose the towers and spire of a
vast convent, revealed by the soft radiance of
the rising moon. We descended to the shore
of the lake, and skirted its quiet waters. The
girl, bearing the pix, her head sunk on her
breast, walked before, without once speaking or
looking round. All was still save the plashing
of the ripples which broke on the shore beside us.

At length we gained the opposite side, and
stood before the convent gate. The girl turned,
and raised her eyes to mine.

"Yours is the only voice that has ever spoken
to me in kindness, the only hand that has ever
been stretched out to do me a good deed. It is

for that that you are alive. Now take this. It is the only thing I possess." And she detached from her neck a small, white carnelian heart fastened to a slender thread of gold. "It is a charm against the evil eye. He threw it to me one night because all the rest were quarrelling for it. With that resting on your heart, you may defy even the eye of Mazitka himself."

I started at the name of that fell astrologer and necromancer, long since hunted by late-roused justice from the bounds of human habitations. I was about pouring out to the girl my gratitude for all that she had done for me; but, turning from me as abruptly as she had addressed me, she sounded the horn which hung by the gate. Its harsh alarum rang far and wide, disturbing the peaceful echoes amid the surrounding hills.

As the clangor subsided, a voice from the wicket asked our errand. But scarcely was the question uttered than it was followed by a scream of astonishment and joy within.

"The pix! the blessed pix! St. Eloi's holy pix!"

And then the voice vanished. In a few moments the gate was thrown widely open, and on the threshold appeared the abbess, surrounded by all the nuns, their glad and excited faces crowding the one on the other under the light of the lamp that swung from the archway, their eyes riveted upon the figure of the girl as she stood supporting the golden pix.

The abbess extended her hand in benediction over the head of the girl, and then the nuns advanced and closed around her. They retreated with her in their midst, and I saw her no more.

The abbess remained alone before me.

I told her my title and my story, and expressed my wish to make a rich endowment to the convent in the name of the young girl who, with the Virgin's aid, had saved me from the peril of a dreadful death. She listened with interest to my tale, and promised that the girl should be gently tended and carefully nurtured in all wisdom and piety. Then she ordered the guest's chamber, in a small building outside the convent walls, to be prepared for me; and, giving me her blessing, she withdrew.

The next morning, I was roused by the sweet voices of the nuns, floating from the chapel windows, as they sang their matin hymn; and my heart was glad within me as I thought of the homeless one who had found shelter, the lonely one who had found eternal love; and I rose refreshed, and, mounting my horse, I proceeded cheerfully on my way.

I rested at mid-day beside a little brook that ran sparkling down through a shady ravine. I freed my horse's head from its heavy frontlet, that it might graze at ease ; and, throwing myself down on the fresh green sod, spangled with little golden cups and pink-tipped daisies, I gave myself up to pleasurable rest.

As I lay dreamily watching the great white clouds piled in majestic repose upon the deep blue of the sky, I heard faint notes of music stealing softly on the air. I roused myself and looked around. Not a human being was in sight; not a trace of human habitation was visible.

" It is some shepherd's pipe," I said. " He gladdens his solitude with these sweet sounds." And again I lay down and listened. The notes poured low but clear upon the air. They seemed, as I hearkened, to take a beseeching tone. I moved restlessly ; my horse stopped grazing, and, his ears bent forward, stood looking intently towards the quarter whence the sounds proceeded. More and more urgent grew the inarticulate tones. Half involuntarily I rose to my feet, and my horse at the same moment moved gently forward. I hastily adjusted his caparisons, and sprang into the saddle. As I did so, the sounds grew sweeter. There was a crystalline joy in them, a happy murmur, as of singing brooks and cooing birds; yet the tones were not those of brooks or birds, — they were human. Whence did they come?

I travelled in their direction all day, and yet they grew no nearer: a rippling stream of delight they passed my ear; hour after hour I pressed on, yet seemed no closer to their source.

The sun went down in purple glory over a swelling horizon of distant hill-tops. The evening star shone clear where the rosy tints of the sky melted into softest blue; yet still the enchanting murmur of the song caressed my ear, and still my steed pressed on to meet the gathering shadows of the coming night. Up the rounded hill-sides, down the grassy valleys, we passed, obedient to the call. The scenery grew wilder as we advanced; the moon, newly risen, showed us the beds of mountain torrents and the sides of barren steeps; yet still we journeyed on. At last, as we passed out from a rugged defile into a plain, the song ceased.

Before me lay the ruins of a city, covering the plain with their irregular masses and broken shadows. High in the centre rose a steep rock crowned with a tower, from whose topmost window streamed a ruddy ray of light.

Much wondering I advanced, threading my

way among the ruins, until I reached the foot of
the rock. Here I left my horse, — for the path
was too precipitous to allow of his ascent, — and
began to climb the broken and uneven steps
which led upward to the tower. There was
something most strange and desolate in the scene
about me as I stopped from time to time to contemplate it. The moonlight streamed over the
ruined walls, and drew their outlines on the grass
beneath. Yawning vaults here and there opened
their pitfalls, and broken columns showed where
once luxurious homes had been reared. All
around the valley was a continuous wall of steep
hills, the defiles between them so narrow that
one man might guard each against an army.

I marvelled as I beheld the desolation that
had fallen upon the city, once so great and so
powerful, as the extent of its ruins showed ; but
a fresher, stronger interest soon chased these
reflections, and again I climbed the precipitous
ascent. At length I reached the summit. I
found myself at the foot of a round tower built
of hewn stone. The only aperture on the lower
story consisted of a heavy door. At this I
knocked. After a long pause I knocked again
more loudly. As I lowered my hand, the door
was slowly opened, and I saw before me the
stooping figure of a man, bent, as it seemed, with

study still more than with years. He held the
door half-open, and stood as if he expected me
to speak my errand and then be gone. A secret
reluctance withheld me from mentioning the
sounds which I had followed until they had
brought me in sight of his tower; and I merely
stated that I was a belated traveller, who requested rest for the night.

The old man shook his head, and without
further ceremony was about to close the door
upon me, when a light step sprang down the
winding staircase behind him, a girlish face
appeared above his shoulder, and a caressing
voice began to whisper earnestly in the ear which
he unwillingly inclined towards it. I thought
that I heard again the music by the brook.

At the urgent entreaty, the hard brow of the
old man relaxed. He opened wide the heavy
door, and bade me enter. The girl came forward
to my side, and, without speaking, slid her small
hand into mine, and led me up the stairs. So
simply and innocently was it done that no tinge
of unmaidenly forwardness seemed mingled
with the act.

Issuing from the dark and winding staircase,
I found myself in a large, circular room. From
the lofty ceiling hung a globe of light which
showed the discordant and unaccustomed objects

around. Ancient bookcases filled with volumes,
some bound in worn and tattered shagreen,
others enclosed in cases of gold and crystal;
stands of narrow shelves, whereon vials of curious shape and design contained liquids of various
tints, some dark and turbid, others in restless
effervescence, and still others clear and pellucid,
— alternated with divans and cushions of rich brocade. High on the walls, as if crawling upward
from the richness below, were fastened dried
crocodiles and hideous serpents; at intervals
dangled enormous eggs, irregularly marked as if
with written characters unsteadily traced; musi-
cal instruments were strewn here and there, and
a cage of brilliant enamel contained a white
dove with a rosy crest. But, in ghastly contrast
to these indications of girlish occupancy, upon
a high pedestal in the centre of the room stood a
yellow skeleton, its eyeless glare and fleshless
grin mocking as it were the luxury around.

On a table near the window was placed a telescope, and beside it were maps and charts covered with figures and signs.

All this my eye took in at a glance; then it
turned and rested upon the old man and the girl:
it rested, and was riveted.

The old man had returned to the occupation
which my summons had apparently interrupted,

and, seated behind the telescope, was already
absorbed in study of the stars. His robe and
cap of black velvet were bordered with purple
fur, such as I had never before seen, and his drapery was held about him by a broad belt of some
curious, semi-transparent material, in texture like
very thin leather.

His profile was turned towards me, and I
could study it without danger of the discourtesy
of attracting his attention. His forehead was
high and narrow, furrowed with lines that ran
transversely towards the centre. His eyes and
eyebrows, cat-like, followed the same line, which
gave a look of singular cunning and perfidy to
his face. His nose was long and aquiline; and
the nostrils, though thin, curved widely outward
at the base, as though perpetually distended by
evil intention. His mouth was small and mea-
gre, its outlines hard and unyielding. . The lips
closed but partially, showing rat-like teeth within. But something which is quite indescribable
was the expression which animated those features. A look so diabolical, of such suppressed
yet exultant wickedness, played over them, fusing
their lines as with a glow of hell, that I felt my
very soul shrink aghast from the contemplation;
and I half resolved to leave the tower at once,
and trust myself to the hospitality of the open

air and the crumbling ruins without. But, as I turned my look upon the maiden, my resolve flickered like the flame of a candle in a sudden breeze, and died out. I had never seen, even in dreams, any thing so marvellous as her beauty, set off as it was by her strange and costly dress.

Her features and figure were of exquisite symmetry; her hair fell in golden waves down to her very feet; her eyes were of deep, transparent blue, soft and pure as a summer lake when not a cloud dims the sky. She was arrayed in some light, fleecy material, as if froth of the sea had been woven and bordered with crimson and gold; and her feet were shod with jewelled sandals, leaving their delicate surfaces bare. Over her whole appearance rested as it were a mist. I looked at her half-blinded, as though I beheld her through the shining spray of a waterfall. Her outlines seemed shifting and unsteady; the only things permanent about her were her deep, soft eyes and the glory of her hair.

She smiled as I looked upon her, and, drawing me to a seat, she unlaced my helmet and bore it away. I could no more resist her than I could have resisted a little child. Then, bringing a small casket, she drew forth some delicious perfume, which she poured upon my hair and my feet. As I inhaled the fragrance, a sense of repose and strength, a quick gayety, ran through me. I felt my color rise and my eyes sparkle.

"Yes, it is so," she said, nodding gently her head. "Now you are no longer tired, you need neither food nor rest. You never inhaled that odor before. It pleases you well."

And, so saying, she drew forward a cushion and seated herself before me, gazing at me with an expression of gentle gladness. She sat some time silent, examining my face with a look of innocent curiosity. At length, "I am glad you have it," she said; and, sinking her voice, she added, "Always keep it, close on your heart."

I gazed at her in amazed wonder. How did this maiden know what had chanced?

"Surely," she answered to my thought, "I know it all."

"How?" I still internally queried.

She replied, "That is very simple. I see when I look; I hear when I listen."

As I gazed at her lovely, shifting face, with its still, sweet eyes, my attention was drawn by a motion in the skeleton behind her. It turned half round on its pedestal, raised its bony hand, and pointed towards a closed window.

"Look there," I said, my eyes fixed upon the fleshless form.

She did not move her head, but replied, "Some one is coming."

Then, rising, she approached the old man. "My father, the slave warns you," she said.

"Who is it?" replied the astrologer, without removing his eye from the telescope.

Looking at her, I then saw a singular change take place in her appearance. All the color died out of her face and figure. She stood thus an instant; then she raised her lids, and the vapory tints returned.

"Rise to meet her," she said. "It is a noble lady from afar."

Unwillingly the old man quitted his telescope, and drew his robe more closely about him, as he prepared to descend.

"Stay, Ombra," he said, turning as he reached the door. "You must not remain here with this brave gallant." And a sneer writhed his wrinkled features as his eye rested for an instant upon me. "When I return, you must be hence."

As he withdrew, Ombra silently unclosed the barred window, through which the skeleton had pointed, and signed to me to follow. She led me up a flight of steps cut in the exterior wall, to the flat roof of the tower. The moonlight fell, still and mournful, on the ruins, drawing a

silver veil of beauty over their decay. Ombra
stood beside me, her crossed hands hanging
before her, her radiant eyes upturned towards
the stars. As I gazed upon her wonderful,
unreal beauty, a thought, a question, arose in
my mind. She answered it gently.

"Yes, it was I that called you."

"Wherefore?" I asked.

"The stars bade me," she replied, still gazing
at them.

"But the stars are silent," I said.

"Nay, their voices fill all space. Do you not
hear them?"

And she raised her hand in the attitude of one
listening.

"What say they to you, O maiden?" I said
in a hushed tone, for I perceived that she heard
them.

"Their song may not be framed into mortal
speech," she replied. "They tell of the mys-
teries that were before the world began, that are,
and that ever shall be. Each in its measure, in
its appointed place, lifts up its voice and sings of
the glory of God, of the marvels of those secret
laws by which Beauty is spread through the
breadth of Creation, and by which Love fills
the loneliness of Space."

She ceased and stood as before, her eyes fixed

on the depths of the sky. I gazed on her and wondered.

"Who, what are you, beautiful one?" I questioned.

"I am Ombra," she answered.

"Your kindred, — where are they?"

"The clouds of the morning, the spray of the waterfall, the dewdrops on the grass, the ripples that sparkle on the sea, — they are my kindred."

"Wherefore dwell you not with them?"

"Because he loves me."

"Is there none else for him to love?"

"None else would dare to love him."

"Wherefore?"

A look of ineffable pity crossed her lovely, shifting face. She turned towards me and said, slowly, —

"*It is Mazitka.*"

At the echo of the dreaded name of that arch enemy of humankind, a chill of horror invaded my every sense. I closed my eyes for an instant. I felt the strength forsaking my members, as if the deadly spell of his eye had been already cast over me. A movement of indignation mingled with and chased my terror as I remembered the witching strain by which I had been enticed to the vicinity of that hoary demon. I turned to my lovely companion with words of reproach upon my lips; but I saw nothing save a form of mist by my side. As I watched, the color returned. She met my indignant look with a gaze of pitying tenderness.

"Listen," she said. "Beside Mazitka sits a woman, tall and fair. Her hair is red and waved, her eyes are black and small, her nose is high and arched, her lips are thin and ruddy. On her right cheek is a crimson mole. Know ye her?"

I felt my flesh creep anew. What horrible mystery lay before me?

"It is my step-mother," I said. "Wherefore comes she hither?"

"It was for this the kindly stars called you," she replied.

And, as she spoke, again her life faded from my sight, and again the mist-like figure stood by me in the silence of the moonlight, and the desolation of ruin around.

Tossed and bewildered as was my mind by the unexpected and sinister events which had befallen me, there was yet one conviction which rose clear and strong upon me, — belief in Ombra, in her will and power to protect and save me. But one dearer than myself, — had she power to protect and save him also, that noble

and honored father, too lofty to think suspicion,
too loyal to dream distrust? As I stood, the
past rose menacing before my memory. I recalled the majestic presence of my father, his
lonely life as he mourned for the young wife
who had died in bringing me into the world;
the hush of the melancholy palace in which my
early years had been spent, and on which the
sun never seemed to shine. Again I saw the
figure of my father's ward, left orphan and pen-
niless by the death of her only parent, accompanied by her duenna, come gliding by my
father's side up the broad staircase of his palace,
the sunbeams that stole timidly through the
heavy windows reflected from her snowy neck
and seeking a prison in the dusky glow of her
curling auburn hair. Again I saw her cat-like
tread as she passed through the stately rooms,
the wily grace with which, as she reached the
suite prepared for her, she thanked him for his
hospitality, and raised his spare, strong hand to
her soft, red lips. And I recalled the look of
furious, smothered hate which she cast on me a
little later, when she heard me say to my father
that Donna Pasquita was not half so beautiful
as the picture of my mother, hanging in the
great saloon.

Ombra's voice broke the chain of my troubled

memories. Turning her face towards the east, again she breathed forth the sweet notes with their persuasive, irresistible charm. Soon a low, rushing sound came from the distance. I saw the trees on the hill-tops which lay to the eastward, bending and swaying. Then I felt the sweep of the wind upon me. It circled around the tower; and it brought to my ear, sharp and distinct, the voices of the speakers within.

"And therefore, fearing this, I would rid myself of him," said my step-mother's voice.

"You have reason," replied Mazitka.

"But no common means will serve me; else I had not travelled so far to seek you," continued my step-mother. "His leech is a crafty and silent man. He doubts me. No drug which may leave any trace must be employed. It must seem some natural disease."

"And the more sudden, the better," rejoined Mazitka.

"The more sudden, the better," repeated my step-mother. And there was silence.

Although as yet no word had revealed it, I felt assured it was my father's death that they were conspiring. I clutched my dagger, and was about to rush in upon them, when Ombra's hand was laid upon mine, and she whispered, —

"Not so. No earthly weapon can harm Mazitka."

"But the woman!" I replied.

"Her hour is not yet come," my companion returned.

Nevertheless, I would have disobeyed her injunction, such was the passion of rage and indignation that possessed me, and the next moment would have seen my dagger deep in the breast of my father's wife, had not Ombra lifted her hand. Immediately I felt myself pinioned by an invisible force that pressed upon me from every side. I could move neither hand nor foot.

"Listen," she said again.

And again I hearkened to the air-borne words.

"A swift paralysis, benumbing brain and members, that shall leave no time for question or misgiving, that shall smite him down even in the midst of his friends, and send him in funeral pomp to join his forefathers."

"It is that, Mazitka: give me that!" she eagerly exclaimed.

"Yes, these are precious drops," he said slowly, after a pause. "Wiser than doctors of law, of physic, and of divinity, they cure all ills alike. The needy heir forgets his stolen birthright; the fevered soldier pines no longer for the sound of the trumpet and the turmoil of the affray; the cowering wretch shrinks no more from the black gulf of the hereafter. In this one pellucid drop there lies the cure for all."

"And it is this!" she said, in a lower tone. "And there is no antidote to be feared, no remedy which may call back life?" she questioned jealously.

"Fear not," he answered. "The drops are distilled from honey. Speedier, deadlier are they than the powder of Trophonius, or the cordial of Liante; nay, subtler even than the essential vapor of Coryatra. For these left traces recognizable by a practised eye, — black spots, or sudden convulsions, or foaming frenzies. But this silent servant works faithfully and discreetly. No grim contortion stiffens the falling corpse; no discourteous blotches betray the secret of the forced obstruction of the vital currents; no telltale drops moisten the forehead of him who is no longer needed. They all die stricken with paralysis, — all, — and they are many."

"And there is no antidote?" she questioned anxiously again.

"None that can avail."

"But I must be safe. I will not tempt fate. I will have no resurrection to destroy me."

"Dread nothing, O courageous lady!" he sneered. "The secret of the antidote is in the keeping of Malaloul. I know it not myself. Fear not that any will go to question her where she sits amid the dead. Now for my counsel. Give it not in secrecy. Spies may dog you; servants may betray you; the leech may come upon you when you are least aware. The only safety is in open hall, 'mid feasting and music and joyful converse. There the light-footed Death can with one finger-tip summon its partner; and all shall see him depart of his own free will and pleasure, regardless of the lamentations of his inconsolable spouse." And the air shuddered with his mocking laugh.

"On the eighth day there is a great festival to celebrate the birthday of my son," she returned. "Search in the horoscope, Mazitka. See if the stars promise favorably for that day."

For a while I heard nothing; then the wind brought to me anew the sound of Mazitka's voice.

"The influences are balanced. All depends on your own firm will and steady brow."

"Then farewell, O Duke Alonso de Guatamarra!" she slowly replied.

It was my father's name!

I listened in vain for more. No further word came to my straining ear.

Presently I saw a veiled figure issue from the shadow of the tower. A man came forth from one of the ruins holding a mule, upon which the woman mounted; and they disappeared in one of the ruined streets which led towards the south.

I looked up to the heavens, half expecting that some sudden bolt of vengeance would fall upon this monster in woman's form; but the stars gazed silently down, registering all in their mysterious archives, but giving no sign.

"Now depart," said Ombra, her deep-blue eyes shining upon me from her lovely, shifting face. "Seek Malaloul. The way lies before you on the west. Pass between the two hills which rise like a cleft cone on the left. Beyond them you will see a mountain, its summit covered with snow. Skirt its base until you come to a cliff on whose brink stands a withered pine-tree. Follow the direction in which it points. You will see a mosque. Enter, and stand in the centre. You will find Malaloul. Say to her, 'Mazitka is at work.' It will be enough."

As she spoke, the astrologer's voice was heard from within calling upon her. As I caught the tone, I wondered mentally why God permitted such an incarnation of fiendish malignity to profane the face of his fair earth.

"He is not all evil," Ombra whispered; "he loves me."

She entered the tower. I followed her. The astrologer smiled as she approached and stood beside him. He cast his arm around her, and drew her nearer. The contact of that fair purity seemed sweet to the mighty wizard.

"My father, the guest must depart," said Ombra.

"What! are you wearied of him already?" queried Mazitka, glancing at me askance.

"He must depart," repeated Ombra. "He waits to say farewell."

Mazitka rose, and turned so as to face me. As his eye fell upon me, the expression of his face abruptly changed. He launched at me a glance which seemed to pierce my very brain; then, with a sudden movement, he leaned forward and caught up my right hand. As he fastened his eye upon the lines of the palm, he uttered a low laugh; then, dropping it, he removed the fur cap from his head, and bowed his tall figure with a gesture of humility which contrasted strangely with the sneering glance that accompanied it.

"Had I known, O puissant young lord, whom it was that I had the honor to receive in my poor dwelling, I should have offered you a different

entertainment.   But since you must needs depart, I wish you good speed on the long journey
that lies before you."

As I stood, my glance riveted upon him, I
saw a singular change take place.   His right
eye grew lustreless and dim ; its eyelid drooped ;
while, at the same instant, the left eye suddenly
expanded. and sent forth a blinding bolt.   It
struck full upon me.   My heart seemed to stop.
A sensation of deadly coldness spread through
my every vein.   I felt my vital forces failing.
But immediately I perceived a current of
warmth proceed from the little carnelian heart
that rested upon my breast.   It flowed, cheering
and invigorating, throughout my frame, chasing
the cold damps that had begun to settle upon my
forehead, and sending ruddy life to every pore.
I breathed again.

Ombra, standing beside the astrologer, smiled
upon me, and with her transparent hand mo-
tioned me farewell.   I gazed one instant upon her
sweet face, with its radiant eyes and changeful
outlines framed in the shining gold of her long
hair, and then I turned away.

I descended the steep and broken steps, and,
mounting my horse, proceeded through the desolate, grass-grown streets, with their long series of
ruined colonnades, their sculptured façades and

fallen gateways, until, leaving the silent city, I passed through the cloven cone of the western hills.

Beyond, glittering in the moonlight, rose the solitary, snow-crowned mountain. I gained its foot, and, skirting its base, I came at length to the broken cliff on whose topmost verge stood the withered pine-tree. Black and riven it towered aloft, and stretched forth a giant arm, pointing across the desert plain. Turning, I obeyed its mute command.

The sandy waste stretched before me as far as my eye could reach. I dismounted and proceeded, leading my horse, which sank above the fetlock in the fine, glittering sand at every step. For several hours we thus toiled on with difficulty. Finally I descried a distant dome before me. With renewed courage I cheered my weary steed, and pressed onward.

As I came nearer, I perceived a Moorish mosque. At a little distance was a graveyard, the sculptured turbans on its tombstones shining brightly in the moonlight. Contrary to the usual Moslem custom, there were no solemn cypresses nor fragrant rose-trees around. Neglect had probably destroyed them long ago.

I ascended the steps, and entered the circular hall within. The delicate arabesques and

13

mouldings of sculptured stone were fresh as if they had just left the cutter's chisel; yet all breathed an air of deep antiquity, of changeless repose. The echo of my own steel-clad foot-steps startled me as they resounded from the moonlit vault above. They seemed a profanation of the weird slumber of Time.

In the centre of the hall lay a large, black marble slab. I advanced and stood upon the stone. It instantly began to sink. I grasped my cross-hilted sword tightly upon my breast, and glanced around. I was sinking into utter dark-ness. I could see nothing save the fast-receding moonlight above me.

The stone was at length arrested in its de-scent. I reached out my hands, and groped in the surrounding obscurity. A narrow passage was before me. I moved onward until I reached its extremity. Facing me was what seemed a solid wall of stone. I passed my hand over its surface. As far as I could judge, it was formed of one enormous block. Exerting all my strength, I pushed violently against its opposing mass. It yielded, and, slowly revolving upon some hidden pivot, revealed the entrance to a chamber within.

The sight before me was not of a reassuring character. I found myself in a low but spacious crypt, dimly lighted by a lamp of bronze which hung from the arched ceiling. In niches around were placed stone coffins. At the upper end of the vault stood a dark sarcophagus. What looked like a heap of loosely piled drapery lay beside it on the ground. I looked around in vain for the sorceress. No human being was to be seen. I called upon her name. There was no answer. Again I called. Nothing but silence replied.

My look unconsciously rested upon the loosely piled heap of drapery, as I stood pondering what was to be my next step. Suddenly I started violently. Two eyes were gazing fixedly at me from out the shapeless mass. As I remained staring upon them like one fascinated, a harsh voice came through the heavy stillness, saying, —

" Wherefore come ye to disturb me, watching beside my dead ? "

The words that Ombra had dictated rose responsive to my lips.

" Mazitka is at work," I replied.

A long, fierce cry broke from the sorceress's lips, and rang circling through the crypt. Each close-sealed coffin seemed to find a voice to echo back that wrathful shriek. She sprang to her feet. Foam flew from her quivering lips ; her eyes darted forth flashes of vengeful light. She shook with the passion of her rage, as a pine-tree trembles in the fury of the storm.

"Ye do well to seek me," she said, when at last her passion began to calm itself. "Now tell me wherein I may defeat his projects, and bring his hated name to shame and scorn."

I briefly recounted to her all. When I had finished, she turned toward the sarcophagus.

"Hearest thou, my father?" she said. "Now shall the faithless fox, the poisonous adder, who crept into thy life, be confounded. Again will I foil him. Again shall thy dead lips smile."

She turned to me.

"Come hither," she said. "Stand where you can see your image reflected in the polished stone. Whatever you may behold, move not, speak not, until the charm be completed."

With that, she placed me so that, reflected on the polished side of the sarcophagus, I saw my own steel-clad figure, illumined by the lamp which hung above.

Malaloul raised her hands above her head, and began to speak rapidly words that I knew not. As she spoke, I beheld my image gradually fading from the mirror. It dimmed before my sight until it had totally vanished. Then she ceased the unknown speech, and said to me, —

"Look on your left hand, but speak not yet."

I looked, and saw myself. Every line of my features, every contour of my limbs, every dint on my armor, every glittering link of mail, all were there. It was my very self. But the eyes were lustreless, and no breath heaved the shirt of mail.

"Stretch out your arm," she said. And, baring my wrist, she punctured a small vein. As the blood sprang forth, she caught it and sprinkled it upon the form.

"Life, give life," she said. And light came to the visionless eyes, and the still lips parted with the living breath.

I stood amazed at what this might portend, but found no words for speech.

Malaloul approached me, and put a little crystal box into my hand.

"Hark to my words," she said. "Journey to the southern border of the plain. This spectre will accompany you. Follow the little river that you will find there, for two days, southward. On the second day you will see, stretched dead beside the water's brink, a monk. Take off his robe, and clothe yourself in it. Then let the spectre mount your horse and precede you. Follow and watch."

"But my father?" I questioned.

" Fear not for any whom Malaloul protects," she answered. " This little box contains a vapor. Let him but inhale it, and the deadly poison wrought from honey shall prove as harmless as water from summer brooks. Life shall return to your father, though he were three times dead ; for this that I give to you is the spirit of that precious fluid for the possession of which kings have offered their diadems, and sages through long centuries have toiled in darkness and stillness in vain."

I would have thanked the sorceress, but she imposed silence upon me with a gesture of her hand.

" Thus much do I," she said ; " and now, in my turn, I lay a charge upon you. The days of Mazitka are shrunken to a span. He is about to sever the golden cord whereon his life has hung. Long have I waited, sitting beside my dead. Long have I studied the star-woven web of fate. I have questioned the serpent of Vishnu, coiled deep in the fiery waters under the middle earth ; I have asked of the tortoise of Odin, in the ice-ribbed caverns beneath the midnight pole ; and the unwearying elephant of Simathin, beneath his everlasting burden, has listened to my voice, and spoken the words of wisdom to my ear. The time draws near. That love

which has protected and saved him hitherto is
dying out. Soon he will stand defenceless.
The hour of vengeance approaches, and then
be ye not far off. I give to you the life ye ask
of me, and ye will repay. Of days a score and
one must pass; then, at the ninth hour, stand at
the door of the tower. Open; the charm will
no longer close the portal against an unfriendly
hand. Ascend the staircase. The slave will
give no sign. Wait and watch. See that your
sword be sharp, and that your arm be strong."

. And, as she ceased, she again took her place
on the ground beside the stone sarcophagus, and
resumed her watch beside the dead.

Side by side with the spectre I passed out into
the subterranean gallery, and the heavy door
closed behind me. I walked on in darkness,
but I heard the measured breathing of the spectre and the sound of his mail-clad footsteps ever
by my side.

At the extremity of the passage the stone still
lay upon the ground. Looking up, I saw the
daylight shining like a star far overhead. I took
my stand with the spectre upon the slab; and
immediately it rose, bearing us upward. We
reached the level of the mosque. The stone
became motionless beneath our feet, fixed firmly
in its place.

As I looked around, my head swam, and my feet refused to support me. The sunlight which streamed through the perforations of the dome seemed blazing into my brain ; the many-hued arabesques danced before my sight in wavering circles. Then for a while there was blackness.

When I again unclosed my eyes, they rested on the spectre of myself, standing with its face turned towards the south, steadily gazing forward. Then all that lay before rushed upon me ; and I arose, and, descending the solitary steps, mounted my horse, and took my way towards the border of the plain. The spectre walked beside me, its eyes ever fixed upon the south.

Strange though it may appear, this unreal companionship had nothing horrible in it. It seemed my settled purpose, clothed with flesh, and become apparent to my sense. It was my *will* that walked beside me over the burning sands, its unswerving look upon the distant south.

At nightfall we reached the border of the plain, and came upon a little, fast-flowing river. Two days more we proceeded, and at sunset we found the monk lying under a thorn-tree close by the murmuring waters. His hands, still warm, were folded on his breast ; the breath had but recently left his frame.

I scooped a grave for him beneath the thorn-tree, and buried him there, after I had drawn from the shoulders which no longer needed its protection the heavy monastic robe.

I clothed myself with it; and, when I had done so, the spectre mounted my horse, and we again journeyed on, the spectre preceding me some twenty stones' cast, silent and steadfast, its face ever turned towards the south.

On the eighth day we entered a deep and gloomy wood, clothing the side of a mountain. The road shrank and became narrow and winding. The sunlight broke but at intervals through the knotted branches above my head; and, as I glanced into the dim recesses on either hand, my eye lost itself in the obscure confusion of black and gray trunks.

I saw by the prints of the horse's hoofs that I was following the spectre of myself; but so dark and so winding was the path that I soon lost sight of both steed and rider.

After some hours of difficult ascent, I suddenly heard a faint cry, as of some animal in distress. At first I paid no heed, but it continued until, moved by compassion, I turned aside to trace it. I found, at a little distance, snared among the bushes, a milk-white kid. It was not struggling. It did not seem frightened, but stood looking about it inquiringly with its large, dark eyes, and at intervals uttering its quavering cry.

I loosed the little creature, which immediately bounded away and vanished amid the woven wilderness of trees. Then I sought to find again the path, but I searched in vain. I wandered till I was weary. At last I saw a broader light, and, making my way towards it, found that I had reached the border of the wood. I stood on a mountain top. Far in the distance lay my native city, beside the silver waters from which it takes its name. I looked eagerly around for the spectre. "Surely it must long ere this have emerged from the wood," I thought.

The road lay level and long before me, descending the mountain side; but no horse or rider was there. As I stood gazing, I saw three armed men of ill-favored aspect issue from the wood, and hurry towards the city. I quickened my pace, and approached them so nearly that I could catch their words. My presentiments had not deceived me. Mazitka had warned my stepmother. These were, in truth, the assassins who had been set to watch for me, to shed my blood almost in sight of my father's house. They were exulting over the rich reward that awaited them, now that their mission was fulfilled.

A shuddering compassion crept over me, an

unreasoning rage. The faithful companion
brought into being, as I now perceived, to receive the death-stroke aimed at my own life, lay
foully murdered within the dark recesses of that
treacherous wood, while I stood whole and un-
harmed, the living tide rushing quick in my
veins, the sun shining bright upon me, the sound
of the summer wind in my ears. I felt as one
whose twin-brother has been traitorously done
to death. I clutched the sword that hung beneath the folds of my monkish robe, and was
about to rush upon the three murderers before
me, when suddenly the air about me seemed
to become vocal, repeating my step-mother's
words, —

"On the eighth day, at even-tide."

I dropped my sword. I had a nearer mission
than to avenge my own wrongs. I clasped the
little crystal box, and hurried on amain.

The road turned at the foot of the mountain,
and led through verdant meadows and fertile
fields, past smiling gardens and cool, still groves.
The murderers, more lightly armed, had out-
stripped me. I lost trace of them in the windings of the road; but, as I followed on, a taint
of blood left by their footsteps seemed to poison
the flower-scented air, and ever before me I saw
a still, dead face, — the face of the spectre, solemn

and steadfast as in its unreal life. My head seemed turning. The words, " On the eighth day, at even-tide," went ringing in my ears. I prayed to the Blessed Virgin, I implored the saints, and still I hurried on amain.

The sun went down behind the soft, green hills; the heavens flamed in purple and gold, then faded into the dimness of twilight. The lights of the city glimmered before me like a giant diadem, sparkling on the ground. I felt neither hunger nor thirst nor weariness, but still pressed on amain.

I reached the city gates. I redoubled my speed as I threaded the streets, swarming with joyous crowds, all swaying in one direction. I heard my father's name on every side. I caught that he feasted that day all the nobles of the city and five hundred poor, in honor of the birthday of his second son. The Duchess, they said, — and they blessed her, — had but the day before returned from her pilgrimage to pray for the Duke her husband's health. And chattering, laughing, and prating, the joyous crowd pressed on towards the palace where that daughter of Sin and Death sat throned beside her trusting lord, — the lord against whose sacred life she was at that instant, perchance, raising her accursed hand.

The crowd gave way before me as I strode on. My religious habit imposed respect; none hindered me, none sought to stay me in my impetuous speed. Panting and breathless, I reached the open square before the palace. It was one blaze of light, one surging sea of human life. I forced my way through its compact mass, and ascended the broad steps, on either side of which blazed great torches above the heads of the assembled lackeys of the guests within. I stood in the great entrance-hall. None knew me in my father's house. Servants were hurrying to and fro, bearing silver and golden platters; the sound of music and feasting came from the banqueting-hall within, and through the open doorway I beheld the gallant array of guests seated around my father's board, whilst from the court-yard below arose a clamorous din, the mirth and rejoicing of the poor as they feasted.

I advanced with rapid strides towards the glittering hall. The seneschal held out his wand to bar my passage.

"The Duke," I said hoarsely, and sought to put aside the wand.

"To-morrow, good father, — to-morrow," replied the seneschal, for he knew me not. "To-night the Duke and Duchess feast their friends.

The revel is at the highest. Ye can have no entrance now."

The words were still on his lips when, sudden and sinister, a many-voiced cry broke from within, and through the blazing portal I beheld the revellers start to their feet in dismay.

I sprang forward. I saw my father fallen back in his chair of state, his face ghastly, his eyes closed. Over him hung my step-mother. The guests were crowding towards him. Cries of affright and lamentation resounded through the hall.

I burst my way through the confused ranks of the revellers; I stood beside my father, and raised that dear head upon my breast; then, holding the crystal box before his nostrils, I crushed it in my hand.

As it shivered in my grasp, a soft, pale flame mounted upward; a faint, delicious perfume spread around; and, blessed be Ombra for ever, the life which had forsaken my father's frame returned. He slowly opened his eyes, sighing deeply, and gazed as in astonishment at the disorder around.

As the glad and wondering exclamations of the guests re-echoed on every side, I raised myself and stood erect beside my father. I turned my face towards my step-mother, and cast from

off my armor the shrouding monkish robe.
Silence fell upon all around. Friends and kindred stood motionless, expectant, scarcely drawing their breath. All felt that some dark tragedy was to be unravelled then and there.

As she beheld me, the Duchess stretched out her palms as if to repel a sight too dreadful to be endured. She shrank back until she reached the wall, and stood there, her eyes, dilated with horror unspeakable, fixed upon me, her white face and marble lips showing in strange and fearful contrast with her flashing jewels and gorgeous robes.

I raised my hand and pointed at her. I knew not my own voice, so hoarse, so deep had it become.

"Pasquita, Duchess of Guatamarra, thrice-perjured wife, unnatural step-mother, I denounce you before God and before the world as murderess and accomplice of Mazitka!"

As I ended, she remained a space motionless in the deathlike silence around; then, slowly sinking to her knees, she fell forward upon her face. No one stirred; no one approached her as she lay, struck down by the revelation of her monstrous guilt. At length, my father, who had so loved her, ordered her women to be summoned. Shuddering, they raised her, and carried her away.

At midnight, cowled forms knocked heavily at the outer gate. It opened. They spoke no word, but silently ascended the broad staircase, and turned towards the Duchess's apartments. When they descended, they bore with them a woman. Never from that time was the name of my father's wife breathed within the walls of the palace; never did she emerge from that midnight into the light of day.

Slowly, in the shrouded gloom of the palace, rolled on the hours until the appointed time of Malaloul's revenge drew near. Then, craving my father's permission, again I took my way towards the ruined city, the home of the astrologer, the dwelling-place of that fair vision who called herself his child. Eight days I travelled on, ever straining my ear to catch the remembered music which had erst called me thither; but silence lay over the blue heavens and over the soft, green earth. No winning murmur rippled past my ear. Ombra's voice was mute.

The time was come. On the ninth hour I stood at the foot of the tower. The moon, red and lowering, hung in the western sky. It cast an angry and foreboding glare upon the dark summit of the tower. A something fearful was in the air. It seemed to choke me. I looked upward. All was dark.

Climbing the broken steps, I reached the heavily clasped portal. It yielded to my touch. A narrow beam shone from a loop-hole, and struck upon the stone wall of the staircase. I stayed not to question it, but sprang noiselessly upward to the circular room. I gently unclosed the door. Within all was changed. Mazitka no longer sat beside the table, studying the mystic circles of the stars. Dust covered the heavy volumes on which I had seen him so intent. The skeleton, with pendant arms and bowed head, stood motionless upon its pedestal. The globe of light above had waned; it shed a faint, uncertain twilight around. The creeping monsters which clung to the walls had roused from their torpor; their flattened and venomous heads were moving restlessly; a pale light was flickering from their eyes.

Ombra was seated on a cushion beside the wizard's former place. Her golden hair lay sweeping the ground; her face rested on her clasped hands. A fainter glow shimmered from the shifting hues of her raiment; the light of her eyes was veiled as though by tears.

I looked around in vain, seeking Mazitka. The room was empty of his hated presence. Suddenly I recalled the beam of light below. I retraced my steps; and, gazing through the loop-hole, unseen, beheld him whom I sought. In a narrow cell, Mazitka stood bending over a roll of ancient parchment. All around him were things ghastly and forbidden, such as my flesh crept to look upon. He had rifled the secret places of the earth; he had disturbed the repose of those great monsters who died before the Flood; he had sought in the caverns of Death for the secret of deathless life; he had ransacked the treasury of prohibited knowledge for that revelation in the search of which he was casting aside his only hold upon existence.

He rose from his stooping posture, and, shaking his head impatiently, turned again to the ancient manuscript. He studied it for a time with a perplexed and frowning brow. Then I saw him carefully examine the margin of the page. As if struck by a sudden thought, he rose hastily, and, seeking a small vial, poured a few drops upon the vacant space. By the pale light of the lamp beside' him I saw some hitherto invisible characters gradually detach themselves from the yellow parchment.

As they formed themselves into words, the necromancer's face grew livid. His white hair bristled around his forehead. Then " Ombra! " broke like a groan from his convulsed, heaving chest. With an abrupt motion he hurled the roll from him, sank into his chair, and pressed his clenched hands before his eyes. Presently he removed them, and sat staring at the empty air before him.

"Avaunt, Death!" he hissed, while he trembled in every limb. "My hour is not yet come." He paused and cowered away, his eyes still fixed as if upon some bodiless presence. A hoarse, rattling sound came from his throat. He shrank as it were into himself until his head was sunk deep between his shoulders. His every feature sharpened as if wrung by some internal spasm. Then, starting to his feet, he cried in a piercing tone that rose into a shriek, "Nor ever shall come!"

With quivering hand he took from the table an object at sight of which my blood froze with horror. It was a sacrificial knife of stone.

He cast his eyes stealthily around him. He bent his ear as if to catch any wandering sound. Then, drawing the folds of his robe closely about him, the monster crept towards a small door, which, opening, revealed a narrow staircase leading upward to the room where Ombra sat.

I bounded up the stone stairway I had descended. I stood again at the door of the circular hall. The dimness of conscious horror brooded within. A pulseless silence weighed on all around. The dying lamp glimmered faintly.

I looked where I had seen Ombra. A fading, mist-like shadow alone met my eye. As I gazed upon it, a little door stole slowly open, and Mazitka crept forth, the fatal knife of stone uplifted in his hand.

The link was severed. The mystic bond gave way. And as Mazitka's footstep, bound on its fell intent, crossed the dark threshold, Ombra, that spirit of light and love, faded before his guilty sight, was resolved into surrounding space, and left him to his doom.

I sprang upon the wizard. My sword was sharp, my arm was strong. I plunged the good steel deep in his accursed heart.

A yell, horrid and drear, broke upon the air. The dying lamp went out; the foundations of the tower heaved and shook beneath me; and from the distance breathed a long, faint sigh.

I raised me from where I bent in the darkness above the lifeless mass that had been Mazitka.

"Ombra!" I called; but no voice replied.

She had vanished utterly and for ever, — vanished to be beheld no more save in the glory of the sunlight, the shimmer of the falling rain, the midnight beauty of the stars: there shall I see her ever, Ombra, fair shadow of a shade.

I quitted the murky blackness of the tower, and remounted my steed. As I left the plain, I turned and looked back. The moon had sunk below the horizon; the stars shone peacefully down over the stillness below; the summer wind rustled softly amid the foliage that clothed the mountain side; the tinkling of a little brook rose from beside my horse's feet. I gazed incredulously around. Had that silent tower ever known an earthly habitant? Had Mazitka been but a delusion? Was Ombra but a dream? And I who have told these tales, — what am I also, save a phantom, unreal, fast fleeting, vanishing even as I speak these words?

Cambridge: Press of John Wilson and Son.

ARTHUR HELPS'S WRITINGS.

1. REALMAH. A Story. Price $2.00.
2. CASIMIR MAREMMA. A Novel. Price $2.00.
3. COMPANIONS OF MY SOLITUDE. Price $1.50.
4. ESSAYS WRITTEN IN THE INTERVALS OF BUS· INESS. Price $1.50.
5. BREVIA Short Essays and Aphorisms. Price $1.50.

From the London Review.

"The tale (REALMAH) is a comparatively brief one, intersected by the conversations of a variety of able personages, with most of whose names and characters we are already familiar through 'Friends in Council.' Looking at it in connection with the social and political lessons that are wrapt up in it, we may fairly attribute to it a higher value than could possibly attach to a common piece of fiction."

From a Notice by Miss E. M. Converse.

"There are many reasons why we like this irregular book (Realmah), in which we should find the dialogue tedious without the story; the story dull without the dialogue; and the whole unmeaning, unless we discerned the purpose of the author underlying the lines, and interweaving, now here, now there, a criticism, a suggestion, an aphorism, a quaint illustration, an exhortation, a metaphysical deduction, or a moral inference.

"We like a book in which we are not bound to read consecutively, whose leaves we can turn at pleasure and find on every page something to amuse, interest, and instruct. It is like a charming walk in the woods in early summer, where we are attracted now to a lowly flower half hidden under soft moss; now to a shrub brilliant with showy blossoms; now to the grandeur of a spreading tree; now to a bit of fleecy cloud; and now to the blue of the overarching sky.

"We gladly place 'Realmah' on the 'book-lined wall,' by the side of other chosen friends,—the sharp, terse sayings of the 'Doctor'; the suggestive utterances of the 'Noctes'; the sparkling and brilliant thoughts of 'Montaigne'; and the gentle teachings of the charming 'Elia.'"

From a Notice by Miss H. W. Preston.

"It must be because the reading world is unregenerate that Arthur Helps is not a general favorite. Somebody once said (was it Ruskin, at whose imperious order so many of us read 'Friends in Council,' a dozen years ago?) that appreciation of Helps is a sure test of culture. Not so much that, one may suggest, as of a certain native fineness and excellence of mind. The impression prevails among some of those who do not read him, that Helps is a hard writer. Nothing could be more erroneous. His manner is simplicity itself; his speech always winning, and of a silvery distinctness. There are hosts of ravenous readers, lively and capable, who, if their vague prejudice were removed, would exceedingly enjoy the gentle wit, the unassuming wisdom, and the refreshing originality of the author in question. There are men and women, mostly young, with souls that sometimes weary of the serials, who need nothing so much as a persuasive guide to the study of worthier and more enduring literature. For most of those who read novels with avidity are capable of reading something else with avidity, if they only knew it. And such a guide, and pleasantest of all such guides, is Arthur Helps. * * Yet 'Casimir Maremma' is a charming book, and, better still, invigorating. Try it. You are going into the country for the summer months that remain. Have 'Casimir' with you, and have 'Realmah,' too. The former is the pleasanter book, the latter the more powerful. But if you like one you will like the other. At the least you will rise from their perusal with a grateful sense of having been received for a time into a select and happy circle, where intellectual breeding is perfect, and the struggle for brilliancy unknown.

Sold everywhere. Mailed, post-paid, on receipt of advertised price, by the Publishers,

ROBERTS BROTHERS, BOSTON.